THE TRUTH ABOUT THE DUKE

WHISPERS OF THE TON (BOOK 5)

ROSE PEARSON

© Copyright 2025 by Rose Pearson - All rights reserved.

In no way is it legal to reproduce, duplicate, or transmit any part of this document by either electronic means or in printed format. Recording of this publication is strictly prohibited and any storage of this document is not allowed unless with written permission from the publisher. All rights reserved.

Respective author owns all copyrights not held by the publisher.

THE TRUTH ABOUT
THE DUKE

PROLOGUE

Why have we stopped?
 The gentleman frowned, looking out of the window though he could not see a great deal, given that dusk had already fallen. "Stanley, might I ask why you have pulled me to so sudden a stop?" The rap on the roof and the call to the driver brought no answer and the gentleman's frown grew heavier, his eyebrows falling low over his eyes as he battled the tension beginning to rise within him. The carriage ride back to his estate had been a long and arduous one and he was more than ready to return home. That journey, however, had now been interrupted though quite for what purpose, the gentleman was not yet sure.

Frowning, he glanced around the carriage, wondering if he had any way of defending himself should it come to it. There was no time for him to consider, however, for there came a sudden cry, followed by a thump which made the gentleman's breath hitch in fright.

Highwaymen.

A cackle of laughter and the sound of his belongings being thrown from the carriage roof only confirmed his suspicions. Frantically, he began to search every inch of the carriage, trying to recall whether or not he had any weapon hidden within. His mind could not fix on any one idea, could not settle on a single thought, his heart racing, his breathing quickening as he searched every inch of the carriage.

And then, he remembered.

Sliding his hand to the back of the seat, he fumbled to find the small gap and, upon securing it, tugged lightly at the seat itself. The entire thing lifted just a fraction, allowing his fingers to close around the small dagger that was hidden there. It was not a pistol, which might have been much more useful given the present circumstances, but it was the only weapon he had.

"And you, my good sir! Are you to show your face to us?"

He did not have time to answer nor even to think of what he might say, for the door to the carriage was swung open for him and a leering face peered up at him. The gentleman's heart threw itself against his ribs as he lurched back as though somehow, hiding himself back into the carriage would help him.

"We are here for your treasures," the fellow said, tilting his head, a kerchief pulled up around his mouth and nose. "You have a fine carriage and you must have something of worth, I am sure."

"Whatever I have belongs to me," the gentleman answered, his voice wavering slightly as he gripped one edge of the seat in an attempt to keep himself steady. "It is not yours to take." Trying to take in the highwayman, trying to make out as many details as he could, the gentleman's eyes narrowed. There was not much for him to see, aside from two flashing eyes and a black hat that was pulled low over the fellow's forehead. The kerchief hid the rest of his features, making it almost impossible to discern anything.

I will remember those eyes, the gentleman told himself, just as the highwayman began to laugh, perhaps discerning his thoughts.

"There is little worth in trying to salvage something – anything – from this," he said, with a chuckle. "You are quite under my control. Your driver has already been conquered by another of my men and as we speak, your things are being laid out for us to search through. Your jewels, however, must be somewhere. And, I suspect, you must have them on your person or in the carriage beside you."

A slight sweat broke out across the gentleman's forehead. The very reason he had gone to London was to collect the family heirlooms which had been sent back to him from the continent. His late father had taken them with him upon his departure from England, though, the gentleman believed, he had not had any intention of dying over there. It had taken months for him to have the heirlooms returned and his delight upon bringing them back to the estate was almost inexpressible.

Save now, that was to be taken away from him.

"I have a good deal of coin on my person, yes." He did not mention the heirlooms, wanting the precious stones to be safe, wanting to do his utmost to hide them from these vagabonds. "There may well be one or two other things in amongst my possessions but – "

"Do you mean to say you have no diamonds?"

The gentleman stopped short, rather astonished by the highwayman's question. How did the fellow know that he had such a thing upon his person? Or was it a mere guess, given his obvious status?

"I asked you a question." The highwayman's voice grew ugly now. "Do you have your diamonds?" When the gentleman did not answer, a flash of a blade was his only warning. The tip pressed lightly against his neck and in that instant, the dagger held hidden in his other hand, seemed utterly useless. He swallowed, his throat bobbing as he tried to answer, his vision blurring just a little.

"The diamonds."

He had no choice but to nod. His life was not worth the heirlooms. To state that he did not have diamonds seemed useless, for what point was there in pretending otherwise? Somehow this fellow, whoever he was, had a clear awareness that yes, he *did* have these in his possession so to lie would only bring him more trouble, he was sure.

"Where?"

The tip of the sword moved away as the gentleman straightened. He gestured behind him, to the boxes tucked away on the floor of the carriage. Pretense would do nothing. They could easily kill him and search the carriage thereafter... though they might very well kill him all the same.

"Fetch them, if you please."

The gentleman swallowed at the knot in his throat, pushing himself back a little as he tried to reach for the boxes all without revealing the dagger. It was foolishness on his part, he knew, but to drop the dagger would make him feel completely vulnerable. To hold it still meant he had a chance – albeit a slim one – to defend himself.

"Here." There were three boxes and, one by one – and with one hand – the gentleman pushed them towards the highwayman. "The diamonds. Just as you expected."

He watched as a flash danced across the highwayman's eyes. Did the fellow realize what it was he had done by revealing his knowledge of these diamonds? He had, whether he had meant to do so or not, shown an awareness of this gentleman: who he was and what he had been about. Though mayhap that did not matter, if his end was soon to come.

"Take them outside." The highwayman lifted his chin. "Then I shall let you and your driver away."

A flare of hope caught his heart but he quickly dismissed it. This man's word could not be trusted. No doubt the sword would pierce him through the moment he had finished putting the last box outside but what choice did he have? Taking a tighter hold of the dagger, he edged closer and, as the highwayman stepped back, rose to his feet so he might step down. The highwayman did not do or say anything, keeping the sword high as the gentleman began to take one box at a time from the carriage. Fear scrambled through his mind as he set the last box on the ground, praying that the growing darkness would give him a chance to escape. His heart hammered furiously, turning his attention to where the driver sat only to see that there was no driver there.

"Where is my man?"

The highwayman chuckled, a tremor raking down the gentleman's spine. "He is indisposed."

But he told me that there were others, the gentleman reminded himself, his eyes beginning to pierce through the gloom a little better now. *Yet I can see none.* Courage began to build within his heart as he glanced all around, the twilight no longer as dark as it had been when he had first stepped out. There was no sound from any other man present, though the gentleman feared what had happened to the driver.

"Going through the rest of your things will not take

long. You will leave them here with me." The highwayman stepped closer, drawing the gentleman's attention. "Now, given that there is nothing else of worth upon your person, I –"

"His rings are gold. Pure gold, I think."

The gentleman started at another voice coming towards him, a shudder of anger tearing from head to foot as he recognized his driver's voice. This had been no accident, then. His driver had, for his own reasons, decided to work alongside this highwayman purely to rob him blind.

"Your rings, then." The highwayman chuckled as the gentleman trembled violently, no longer afraid but filled with a coursing anger. "And anything else you have of worth. There is no point in hiding anything from me."

Recognizing that he could not hide the dagger any longer, the gentleman did the only thing he could think of. Using surprise as his weapon, he sprang towards the highwayman, dagger slashing through the air. It connected with the fellow's face, ripping his kerchief, but the gentleman did not stop there. Slamming it hard into the fellow's shoulder – not quite where he had wanted it to go – he heard the howl of rage and pain that broke from the highwayman's lips, coupled with the roar of fury from the driver behind him.

Then, he ran. With unsteady legs, he forced himself forward into the darkness. He heard the driver shouting, the highwayman's cry of agony as, no doubt, he wrenched the dagger from his shoulder, but those sounds only forced him forward all the faster. Chest heaving, he slowed for just a moment, hearing a quiet nicker nearby.

His horse!

Blinking furiously as he slowed to a walk, the gentleman's eyes slowly made out the shape of a horse and, with hope beginning to build, made his way towards it. The reins were looped over a tree branch, his fingers slipping as he fought to free the creature. He did not doubt that the driver was coming in search of him now, perhaps the highwayman also. If he was found, death would be the only end. With a cry of relief breaking from his mouth, he freed the reins. Placing one foot in the stirrup, he pulled himself into the saddle, kicking hard into the horse's sides.

A shout from just behind him sent a wave of realization crashing into him, seeing just how close he had come to being caught. Sweat ran into his eyes and he blinked it away, pushing the horse to ride further into the darkness of the night. The horse did as he was bade, perhaps used to the gloom and the chill. With relief beginning to pour through him, the gentleman realized that safety was now within reach.

I will have to hide until the morning dawns. A chill began to whisper around his shoulders as he slowed the horse to a trot, having very little awareness as to where he might be. *They could come searching for me.*

Nodding to himself, he glanced up at the sky, praying silently that the clouds would part for him and the moon shine its brightness out onto the road all the more clearly. Seeming to hear his inner thoughts, the clouds slowly began to shift and the gentleman's heart slowly began to settle.

Yes, the diamonds – his heirlooms – were gone, but he was alive and well. That was all that mattered.

Though how had the highwayman known of his diamonds? What had led his driver to connect with such a nefarious person? Questions upon questions began to flood the gentleman's mind though, no matter how long he considered and how far he rode, none brought with them any answers.

CHAPTER ONE

And thus, it begins... just as I suspected it might.
Henry set a smile to his lips as he was greeted by not one but three young ladies, all of whom batted their eyes at him and sent brilliant smiles in his direction. A chorus of, 'Good evening, Your Grace' met his ears and he was forced then to try and recall the names of the three young ladies before him. They had already been introduced, though Henry could not recall any of them. And this when he had only been in London society for a few days!

"Good evening to you all." Bowing, he lifted his head and kept his smile pinned. "I do hope you all are enjoying the evening? You all must be delighted at the crush of guests here this evening! There are plenty of gentlemen for you all to dance with." Wincing inwardly at just how many times he had said, 'you all', Henry cleared his throat, aware of the heat in his face.

"Oh yes, we are indeed!" One of the young ladies, with her bouncing curls, beamed back at him. "We are very glad to have so many offers to dance."

"I am sure that you are." The warmth increased as he

silently cursed his foolishness at mentioning the dancing. It was clear now from the eager, expectant looks on the ladies' faces, that they were now waiting for him to ask for their dance cards. And this when he had not any intention of dancing at all! When he did not do as they so obviously expected, the three young ladies all exchanged glances, their smiles slipping a little. The second young lady, the one with clear blue eyes, tilted her head in a coquettish manner, her lips pulled into a overly bright smile.

"If I might be so bold as to ask, Your Grace, are you to dance this evening?"

"I – " Henry spread out his hands, wishing that he had some legitimate excuse as to why he could not do such a thing. "I suppose that I – "

"Good evening, Your Grace!"

With searing relief, Henry turned to greet his good friend, the Marquess of Kendall, to the conversation. "Good evening, Lord Kendall!" His voice, he realized, sounded a little overly enthusiastic and he tempered it quickly. "Have you just arrived?"

Lord Kendall nodded though his gaze lingered on the three young ladies. "Yes, I have. My sister and her husband came for dinner and we lingered much too long over the port!" He laughed at this, making Henry grin but this came solely from the fact that the young ladies were showing more interest in Lord Kendall now, rather than turning their attentions back towards him. Mayhap, he considered, he would be able to escape from the clutches of the three young ladies and permit the Marquess to dance with them all instead!

"The Duke was just asking us about dancing." The third young lady, one who had not spoken as yet, turned her enquiring eyes back towards Henry, making his spirits – and his hopes – sink sharply. "It is a very fine ball and we should all like to dance as many dances as we can this evening!"

The other two ladies giggled, though one made a quiet comment about how her friend was being a little too bold in her remarks, though that did not seem to stop her from turning eager eyes towards Henry again. Sighing inwardly, Henry threw a look to his friend, though the Marquess only lifted an eyebrow and did not otherwise speak.

"Yes, of course." With a smile that he did not feel, Henry gestured to the third young lady. "Your dance card, if you please?"

"Miss Halethorpe, you *must* grant me the dance card thereafter. And you both also, Lady Annette, Lady Beatrice. Only if you wish to oblige us, however." With a grin, Lord Kendall not only helped Henry remember the titles of the three young ladies but also gained fawning looks and delightful smiles for himself. Still a trifle irritated that he would have no other choice but to dance with them all, even though he had very little desire to do so, Henry took one card after the other and chose three that came one after the other. That way, he could make quite certain that the dances were over and done with as quickly as possible, leaving him free to do as he pleased for the rest of the evening.

"There now." Taking the third card from him, Lord Kendall quickly signed his name and then returned it to Lady Beatrice. "We shall all have the pleasure of being in each other's company again very soon."

"Thank you, Lord Kendall. And you also, Your Grace." The one that Henry now knew to be Lady Annette, turned her gaze back towards him rather quickly, a flash in her blue eyes. "One must wonder which young lady the Duke of

Melrose shall dance the waltz with this evening. It is to be none of us, I see."

Henry blinked, then tried to laugh the comment aside, for it was, to his mind, much too bold for a young lady to say and he had no intention of answering it.

"It shall remain a mystery, I think!" Seemingly ever the rescuer, Lord Kendall spoke up again and then inclined his head. "Alas, we must take our leave for I can see three gentlemen approaching with the clear intention of coming near to you three ladies. Until later this evening."

Henry turned away without so much as a nod to the ladies, relief in his veins as he walked alongside Lord Kendall. "Thank you, my friend."

Lord Kendall chuckled, leading Henry to the door which led to the refreshment room. "I could see that you were already looking a little overwhelmed by their presence. I do hope you noticed the several other ladies who were slowly pressing towards us. That is, *before* I took you to the refreshment room and away from them!"

Henry scowled, making his way to the table that was set with an array of liquor, though he quickly turned away from the watered-down ratafia and picked up a glass of punch instead. "I did not expect to be so... sought out so quickly."

"Did you not?" Lord Kendall's eyebrows lifted. "I did warn you only a few nights ago that society would be delighted – nay, *overcome* – by your presence here, did I not? You are a Duke! You hold the highest title in all of England aside from the King, and with great wealth too with your standing, is it any wonder that the young ladies of society seek you out?"

"I wish they would not," Henry grumbled, his jaw jutting forward. "I should like to be able to find a young lady without so many *presenting* themselves to me."

Lord Kendall snorted at this, rolling his eyes as Henry's grimace deepened. "You are utterly ridiculous, my friend. You cannot expect to walk into a ballroom and be ignored by the young ladies of society *and* their mothers, I might add. Though, I might wonder if you have a specific young lady in mind?"

Henry took a sip of his punch, then shook his head. "If you are asking me whether I have found a young lady to interest me already, then the answer is no."

"But you have an understanding of what it is precisely you are searching for when it comes to making a match." Lord Kendall tipped his head just a little, his dark eyes questioning. "After all, that is why you are here, is it not? To make a match?"

"Yes." Having already explained himself to his friend at their first meeting, Henry shrugged. "I must marry. The heir must be produced and that is the only way for such a thing to come about. However, the young lady that I choose for my bride must be a good many things, which is why I dislike being pressed so by so many."

"Because you cannot distinguish one from the other."

"In part, yes." Henry took another sip of the punch, gesturing to the door that led back to the ballroom. "The young ladies of London are demanding in their attentions, I find. One of them this evening – Lady Annette, mayhap? – was *much* too forward in some of her speech and her manner! That, I suppose, would make me unwilling to proceed with even calling upon her to take tea, but the other two I might consider. Though I suspect that I shall find them both sorely lacking when it comes to my requirements."

Lord Kendall spread out his hands on either side. "Which are... ?"

"Just as every gentleman might want," Henry answered with a shrug. "She is to be of a high standing, of course. There must be an amiability about her, though she ought to be gentle in her manner and her speech. I should not like to have a wife who speaks her mind without even a thought!" He waved one hand in his friend's direction. "You know the sort of thing I mean."

"Genteel without being brash or demanding, yes."

Henry nodded, a sense of satisfaction in his heart that his friend understood him so well. "I should like her to be respectful, to understand her situation and her standing without having even a *hint* of arrogance and pride. She must be able to manage a household, though with a quietness of nature in doing so for I should not want a wife screeching and screaming at the housekeeper and the maids!" Warming to his subject now, he continued with even greater feeling. "I should prefer that she be able to play the pianoforte very well, though I would settle for the harp. Painting, needlework, and the like are of no interest to me though I do want her to have some hobbies of her own that do not require my presence or my involvement in any way. She must not have any desire to press me when it comes to my time and should have no expectation that we should always sit for dinner together and the like. It is important to me that my duties come first and a Duchess must understand that." Finishing, he drained his cup of punch and then went to pick up another, a little surprised to see that Lord Kendall's jaw had gone a little slack. "Is there something wrong?"

His friend blinked once, twice, then ran one hand over his jaw. "You have quite astonished me, Melrose."

Henry frowned. The expression did not come from his friend's lack of 'Your Grace', for their friendship had been since boyhood and Henry considered Lord Kendall to be almost a brother in that regard. Rather, it came from the confusion over why his friend should *be* so astonished, especially when there was nothing to be surprised about.

"You do not understand why I am so." Evidently seeing Henry's confusion, Lord Kendall shook his head and then offered a wry smile. "I shall explain. Your list of requirements for the lady who shall be your bride is not only ridiculously long but has so many high standards fixed in place that I fear you shall not find a lady who can secure them all!"

"Nonsense." Henry looked away, ignoring the twist of unease in his stomach. "I am sure there will be many young ladies who will be able to do all that I ask and fulfill all that I require."

"I shall be greatly surprised if it is so," came the reply. "I do not think that any young lady in all of England would be able to answer everything you have set out! Indeed, I think such an idea is nothing more than an imagination."

Henry shook his head firmly. "I am quite sure you are wrong."

"You truly believe that you will find a young lady able to meet all your requirements and standards without even a modicum of failure?"

Trying to build his confidence despite his friend's remarks, Henry stood as tall as he could. "I am quite certain of it."

Lord Kendall chuckled, his eyes dancing. "If I were a betting man – and if we were in Whites – then I would place a wager that you, despite all your determinations, will end up falling in love with either a bluestocking or a wallflower!"

At this, Henry shuddered, making Lord Kendall laugh

all the more loudly. He scowled, suddenly a little irritated at his friend's response. "I do not know what you find so funny about that statement. That would be the most dreadful circumstance imaginable!"

With a snort, Lord Kendall rolled his eyes. "I hardly think so, my friend. To fall in love is, I think, quite a wonderful situation."

"But not one that I desire for myself," Henry stated, firmly. "I have no intention of letting any sort of emotion cloud my judgment. I will not let myself feel even a sliver of attraction or interest towards any young lady, for then I shall quite lose myself and, no doubt, make a great mess of all that I have determined!"

Lord Kendall came a little closer to Henry and, much to Henry's irritation, set one hand on his shoulder and spoke in an almost fatherly tone, as though to suggest that Henry had very little idea as to what he was saying.

"My friend, to fall in love is the very thing I am striving for and certainly, to my mind, is not something that ought to be mocked."

"I do not mock it," Henry answered, a little sharply, "but I state only that it is nothing that *I* desire for myself, for I see no worth in it!"

"Then you are mistaken." Lord Kendall dropped his hand and smiled wryly. "I know that my statement frustrates you but you shall not take the hope of love and affection from my heart."

Henry lifted his chin. "And you shall not take the hope of finding a suitable young lady to fulfill my requirements from me either."

Letting out a sigh, Lord Kendall looked away. He did not speak for some minutes and Henry's shoulders slowly lowered, recognizing the tension that had been built between himself and Lord Kendall. Tension that he did not wish to linger.

"It is not something that we need discuss again." Lord Kendall turned back towards Henry, who quickly nodded. "We both have very different expectations, do we not?" He tipped his head. "Do you think you shall tell your young lady – whomever she may turn out to be – about the missing heirlooms? A wife might expect to be able to wear the family jewels one day."

Henry grimaced. "No, I do not think I need to. That is a story from the past and, besides which, I have plenty of other jewels which she might wear, should she so desire it."

Lord Kendall nodded slowly. "I suppose that is wise." He smiled. "I will not ask you about such a thing again. I know that it is a source of frustration to you."

"It is, but that is solely because I do not know what happened to them!" Henry sighed and shook his head. "My father only told me that they were lost and any further explanation was never given. It does make me feel a little *less* of a gentleman to have no heirlooms to give to my bride but I am certain she will understand."

A gleam came into Lord Kendall's eye. "Unless *her* requirement for a husband is that she have diamonds given to her on her wedding day." Seeing Henry's scowl, Lord Kendall winced and then laughed, forcing Henry's lips to curve regardless. "Forgive me, I have already said that we will not speak of it again and here I am making light of it all! We have differing expectations, as I have said, and that is quite all right."

"Indeed, but that does not mean that one is better than the other," Henry answered, reaching out to shake Lord Kendall's hand. "I do not want to damage our friendship because of this."

Lord Kendall grasped his hand firmly. "Nor do I." He smiled as he released Henry's grip. "Let me say, however, that I shall do what I can to support you in your endeavors, despite my thoughts on your list of requirements."

Henry grinned, relieved that the tension had melted away. "Thank you, my friend. I would state that I could do the very same to support you but alas, I feel as though my understanding of such things is limited and will do nothing but cause trouble and confusion, were I to attempt it."

With a guffaw, Lord Kendall reached for another glass of punch. "Indeed! I value your willingness, certainly, though I think it would be best if you did nothing whatsoever when it comes to my search for a young lady to fall in love with."

"Then it is settled," Henry answered, as they both began to make their way back to the ballroom. "And let us hope we both find success by the end of the Season. I do not think that I can endure another London Season such as this one and I have only been present in London for less than a sennight!"

Lord Kendall laughed aloud again and Henry's grin lingered, though inwardly, he could do nothing but think of what his friend had said about love.

I must pray that I will never have even an inkling of affection when it comes to my search for a bride, he thought, his eyes running over the crowd of guests before him. *That would be the very worst situation I could ever find myself in, I am sure.* His scowl slowly returned as he considered what would happen should he find his heart affected. *It must never happen. And I must do all that I can to prevent it.*

CHAPTER TWO

"But you know that I have no desire to attend the ball!"

Lady Hampshire sighed loudly and turned her head away in clear frustration. "Lydia, I will hear no more of your complaints! Your father and I are well aware that you have no desire to be present here in London, that you have no interest in being presented to the King and you do not want to be a part of society. We have heard it from you almost every day since the very first moment that we stated it was to be your come out. Yet still, you do not seem to understand that what you do not desire is to come about regardless of your feelings on the matter!"

Taking in her appearance, Lydia let out a quiet sigh, trying to tell herself that her protests would, in some way, make a difference even though – as her mother had only just pointed out – they had not done anything as yet. The cream gown was not a color that suited her, she considered, given her reddish curls and green eyes. Yet, it was the only one that her mother would consider Lydia wearing, despite her complaints. Apparently, a debutante did not wear anything other than pale colors, though Lydia herself would have much preferred a dark shade of green or some such thing.

"Now." Her mother came towards her and took her hands in both of hers, a stern look in her eyes. "You will listen to me, Lydia, or I will have your father come to speak with you."

Lydia shrunk just a little, fully aware that her love of learning, of reading and exploring, was not something that her father had ever encouraged. The only person she had ever had to champion her in that way had been her elder brother, Rupert. Though given that he had recently married and taken hold of his own estate, Lydia had no one to support her. She felt the loss of his presence keenly, especially in moments like this.

"Your father and I have expectations of you, my dear." Even though her mother spoke kind words, there was no softness in her tone, no gentleness or even a hint of understanding. "You are *not* to do anything that would make anyone here in London realize how much of a bluestocking you are. Do I make myself quite clear?"

Lydia nodded, turning her head away.

"You are to speak *only* when spoken to, you will acknowledge and greet every gentleman and lady that you are introduced to in the correct manner and you will not let a single word about your recent... " Her lip curled in distaste. "Your recent *learning* come of your mouth."

"Yes, Mama."

There was nothing more for Lydia to say but to agree. Arguing with her mother would do nothing and she had to acknowledge that her complaints were gaining her no ground either.

Though I do not intend to permit her to continue to

guide my every step, she considered, as her mother wittered on just how little Lydia cared for propriety and how learning and reading extensively was not something that a young lady ought to be pursuing. *I will find a way to make as much enjoyment of society as I can, despite these less than delightful circumstances.*

"Are you listening to me?"

Lydia started lightly, then looked back at her mother. "Yes, of course. I have every intention of doing as you have asked."

Her mother shook her head and sighed before stepping away, making for the door, and then throwing a glance towards Lydia, clearly expecting her to follow. With a nod, Lydia hurried after her, fully aware that her mother's ire was already raised.

"Your father is waiting in the carriage already, and he knows very well what I have said to you before our departure," Lady Hampshire continued, as they walked along the hallway to the open front door. "Do not think to let either of us down this evening, Lydia. Or it will be all the worse for you."

"Yes, I have some dances still remaining." Lydia's jaw tightened as she kept her smile fixed. "Thank you, Lord Bridgemouth. You are very kind." She dared a glance at her mother as she spoke, relieved to see that there was a small smile on her face rather than the glower she had been wearing thus far.

"How delightful!" Lord Bridgemouth – a gentleman with such a sharp nose that Lydia had trouble not staring at it – bent his head low and then wrote his name on her dance card. "I do always look forward to dancing with the young ladies, particularly the debutantes."

"Is that so?" A little surprised – and slightly worried – but that certain remark, Lydia lifted an eyebrow. "And why might that be?"

Lord Bridgemouth grinned but it was not a pleasant smile. "Why, it is a pleasure to step out with such innocent young ladies, those who have never stepped out in society before. It brings me a sense of contentment to show them some of what London society is about."

"Mmm." Lydia tilted her head, her eyes narrowing just a little. "I must say, I – "

A hand set onto Lydia's shoulder, fingers digging into her skin. "That is so very kind of you, Lord Bridgemouth. I am certain that a good many debutantes are grateful to you for such a kindness." Lady Hampshire pressed her fingers all the more tightly and Lydia fought not to wince. "My own daughter included."

"Yes, indeed," Lydia managed to spit out, though her smile was no longer present given the pain her mother's fingers were pulsing through her shoulder. "I look forward to our dance, Lord Bridgemouth."

The gentleman beamed at her, clearly entirely unaware of all that Lydia had been about to say and the questions she had been about to ask. Turning away, he walked to the very next young lady near to them and Lydia rolled her eyes, before snapping them back into place as her mother's hand finally lifted.

"Lydia, what did I tell you?" Hissing out of the corner of her mouth, the Countess swung around to face Lydia. "You are not to – "

"Lydia? Is that you?"

A familiar voice sent a flurry of relief through Lydia as

she turned on her heel, ignoring her mother in an instant as she flung her arms tightly around her friend – and quickly heard her mother tut disapprovingly.

She did not care.

"Sophie! How glad I am to see you!"

Sophie, now Lady Markham, grasped Lydia's hands tightly, her eyes shining. "Not as glad as I am to see you!"

"I did not think that you would be in London this Season!" Lydia exclaimed, still ignoring her mother's presence. "After your marriage last summer, I thought you would be enjoying summer at Lord Markham's estate!"

Her dear friend smiled. "My husband is to bring his sister into society and make certain she finds a match. Thus, I am here in London again and overwhelmed with delight and joy at seeing you again! We have so much to talk about, so much to share, I am sure!"

Lady Hampshire cleared her throat and Lydia closed her eyes briefly, her happiness beginning to evaporate.

"Good evening, Lady Hampshire." Lady Markham dropped into a quick curtsy, a warm smile on her face. "I must apologize for my lack of greeting, I was so caught up with delight in seeing Lydia again!"

A hint of a smile touched the edge of Lady Hampshire's lips, though it quickly dropped. "Of course, Lady Markham. I do hope you have settled into your husband's estate?"

"I have, yes." With a warm smile, Lady Markham glanced at Lydia, jerking her head just a little to the left as Lydia began to smile, understanding what her friend meant for her to do. "And since I am now wed, I would be *very* glad indeed to help chaperone Lydia. My husband is well acquainted with many of the gentlemen here in London – the unattached ones, I mean – and I would be able to make many excellent introductions."

"How *very* kind of you, Sophie!" Lydia exclaimed, looping her arm through her friend's before her mother even had a chance to protest. "I shall return with my dance card quite full, I am sure."

She stepped away quickly, hearing her mother splutter behind her but much to Lydia's relief, nothing more was said or done to prevent her from taking her leave. They had only taken a few steps when Lydia let out a burst of laughter, quickly joined by Sophie.

"You did *very* well, my dear friend," Lydia giggled, as they both continued to weave their way through the crowd. "You are clearly very well aware that I have no interest or desire to be in company with my mother on this occasion!"

"I am sure that you have no desire to be at this occasion or any other occasion, is that not so?" Sophie lifted an eyebrow as Lydia winced. "You are still just as much of a bluestocking as ever."

Lydia slowed her steps just a little. "And you are not?"

Her friend chuckled softly. "I am, of course."

"And your husband still does not mind that you are just as eager to learn and study as he?" Lydia's heart ached desperately as her friend nodded, seeing the smile on her lips and wishing that she too might have had the same freedoms as Sophie. They had known each other from childhood, for Sophie's father, the Viscount of Althorpe, was close friends with Lydia's father, the Earl of Hampshire. They were almost like sisters might be, sharing the same interests and hobbies and, with that, an ever increasing friendship. The only difference was that Sophie's good parents had been quite contented to have their daughter learn and study but Lydia's parents had behaved as though Lydia was stricken with some sort of malady. Thus, she had been forced to hide her books, to do what she could to prevent them from discovering just how much of a bluestocking she was... though her education provided her with wisdom, understanding, and a knowledge of present circumstances within the world that could not be hidden away no matter how much she tried.

"Your mother and father still dislike all that you have become?"

Lydia gave her friend a small, sad smile. "You still can read my thoughts, it seems. Yes, in answer to your question." She closed her eyes for a moment, waiting for the wave of sadness to crash over her. "They have warned me that I am not to speak a word out of turn during my time here in London, though quite how I am to marry a gentleman who does not know the truth about who I am, I cannot imagine."

Her friend reached to press her hand. "I am sorry. That must be a difficult struggle for you." The edge of her lip curved upwards. "Though I expect that you do not have any intention of doing what it is that they ask of you."

Lydia grinned, her sadness quickly evaporating in the light of being in the presence of someone who not only understood her but valued her desire to learn. "You are quite correct there, my friend. No, I have no intention of behaving as they expect me to. I shall upset them should they discover it, but now that I have you by my side, I must hope that I will be able to do as I please as often as I can!"

"So long as your mother permits it?"

Lydia's smile grew. "As often as I can slip away from her, then yes. And I have every intention of doing so just as often as I can."

"Where have you been?"

Lydia ignored her mother's sharp remark and lifted her

chin just a little. "My dance card is almost full, Mama. Are you not pleased?"

This seemed to take some of the fury from Lady Hampshire's frame, for her shoulders dropped almost at once and the tight slash that had been her lips softened.

"Should you like to see?" Lydia held out her dance card for her mother to see, noticing how Lady Hampshire's eyes widened. "Sophie was as good as her word."

"I can see that." Lady Hampshire's voice had quietened now, her eyes still holding a little surprise. "I did not think... well, that is good. Though I have *just* heard that there is a Duke present this evening and I am determined to have you introduced to him."

Lydia's shoulders slumped. Sophie had done just as she had promised in introducing Lydia to various gentlemen, though she had been very careful in her selection. The gentlemen that were now listed on Lydia's dance card were all those who Sophie considered to be both genteel and understanding, given that they might one day learn of Lydia's love of learning and the like. Her mother, on the other hand, would introduce her to any and every gentleman – the higher the title, the better – rather than have any consideration for the sort of gentleman that her daughter might prefer.

"The Duke of Melrose is his name." Lady Hampshire leaned a little closer to Lydia, her eyes sharp. "And you will behave with the *utmost* propriety, Lydia. Else you will be whispered about by all of the *beau monde* and bring shame to not only yourself but also to your family name."

Lydia scowled. "I have no intention of bringing shame to anyone, Mama. I simply wish to be myself."

"And yet, you shall not be permitted to be so." Lady Hampshire looked all across the room, her hand snaking around Lydia's arm. "There he is, now. Come, I can see that Lady Newton is speaking with him and since I am acquainted with her, she will be able to introduce us!"

There was no choice but for Lydia to go along with her mother's intentions, being half pulled through the crowd of guests as Lady Hampshire walked with determination towards the Duke. Lydia managed to make him out, seeing that he stood almost half a head taller than the other gentlemen near him. The closer she came, the more her instincts turned against this fellow. Yes, he might well be a Duke and with the highest title in all of London, but it was clear to her, she considered, that he was arrogant and superior. The way he let his gaze rove around each and every face near to him, the way his lip curled just a little, his chin lifted – did that not speak of haughtiness and condescension? Yes, he was handsome – as every Duke should be – but his manner alone turned her away from him.

"Oh, is that you, Lady Newton?"

Lydia rolled her eyes at the way her mother spoke, hearing the feigned surprise and the tinkling laugh that followed it. As she did so, her eyes lit upon the Duke of Melrose for just a moment and caught the way he looked at her. His eyebrow was lifted, clearly surprised that she would do such an unladylike thing as to *roll her eyes* when in company.

That only made Lydia want to do so again.

"Lady Hampshire, how wonderful to see you!" Lady Newton bobbed a curtsy and then gestured to the Duke and the gentleman beside him. One who appeared to be a good more amiable given the way he was smiling, a gentleness in his expression. "I was just speaking with the Marquess of Kendall and the Duke of Melrose. Are you acquainted with either of these fine gentlemen?"

"No, I am not. And nor is my daughter." Lady Hampshire gestured towards Lydia, only for another gentleman to hurry towards them all.

Lydia smiled broadly, inwardly thrilled that she now had an excuse *not* to be introduced to the arrogant Duke. "Viscount Glenville! Is it our dance already?"

Lord Glenville, a gentleman with a shock of dark hair and a rather youthful face, beamed at her, perhaps delighted at her eagerness. "Yes, Lady Lydia, it is."

"Oh, but I was just about to – "

"I cannot have Lord Glenville left waiting, Mama," Lydia answered, though she kept her voice low so as not to be overheard by the Duke, Lord Kendall, or Lady Newton. "We might miss our dance entirely! I shall return to you the moment this dance is at an end, of course."

She did not wait but stepped away with Lord Glenville at once, silently triumphant. Her mother's intentions to introduce her to various gentlemen had, for the moment, been foiled and the rest of the evening would be spent in the company of gentlemen who might not view her bluestocking ways with as much dislike and disinclination as her very own mother and father! Throwing a glance over her shoulder, Lydia caught the Duke of Melrose's heavy frown, perhaps displeased that she had dared to set aside an introduction to him in favor of a Viscount but she did not care in the least. With a smile on her face, she was led towards the dance floor and, as it quickly began, set all thoughts of the Duke of Melrose from her mind.

CHAPTER THREE

"You look... displeased."

Henry glowered at the host for the evening, a little irritated that he had come to break through the silence he had surrounded himself with, though inwardly he knew he had no right to do so. Lord Dunford had been a friend of Henry's late father though Henry did not know him particularly well himself. "Not at all, Lord Dunford. I am not in the least bit displeased, though I was very much appreciating the quiet of the library."

"And why is that?" Lord Dunford asked, his face wreathed in smiles and not in the least bit concerned about Henry's melancholy mood. "You are at what I hope will be one of the most excellent soirees in the Season and you state that you are enjoying the quiet?" The smile faded as he ran his hand over his beard, a frown on his forehead. "Something must be wrong."

Indeed it is.

Henry could not quite place a finger on what it was that troubled him but these last two weeks in London had made him a little... disappointed. He had not wanted to admit anything to Lord Kendall but part of him feared that, had his friend made the bet he had threatened, then he might now be well on his way to winning.

"It must be a little overwhelming for a gentleman in your position," Lord Dunford continued, with a small smile. "A Duke, coming to London to seek a wife! I well recall your father doing the very same thing! Though he was quick to make his match, however." His smile grew a little sympathetic. "I am sure that almost every young lady in London has been introduced to you by now."

All but one.

In an instant, the young lady that had practically shunned him to go and dance with a mere Viscount flashed into Henry's mind. It had been a little over a sennight since that had taken place but it had not left Henry's mind, no matter how much he had attempted to fling it from himself. To be so ignored had been most displeasing and yet, the young lady had seemed almost glad to be free from her introduction to him! He had caught the way she had glanced back over her shoulder towards him, had seen the flickering smile that had followed soon afterward, and had felt his ire grow strong.

Though, it was quite foolish to be so irritated, he had reminded himself on more than one occasion. He had met many a young lady, so why should he care if only one of them was not in the least bit eager to be introduced?

"You are sober minded indeed!" Lord Dunford frowned. "If it would be helpful, I could permit cards to begin a little earlier than I had otherwise anticipated." Lord Dunford spread out his hands, though Henry quickly shook his head. "I do want you to be quite at home here this evening, and if cards would assist you then I would be glad to have it all set up at this very moment!"

"Oh, I am quite comfortable, I assure you, there is no need to make any changes." Seeing that Lord Dunford was clearly a little concerned for him and, in his own mind, a little worried that such concern might be spoken of to others, Henry quickly smiled. "You are quite correct to state that it can be, at times, a little overwhelming when all of society knows that one is looking for a suitable match! And not to mention that I have been written about in The London Chronicle on more than one occasion."

Lord Dunford chuckled ruefully. "I have seen that, I will admit. It is, I confess, some gentleman's dream to be written about in such golden terms as you have been!"

Henry smiled briefly. "It is perhaps something I ought to consider in a different light." He took a breath. "But I should return to the soiree. There is to be some excellent entertainment this evening, is there not? I have heard that you have planned something excellent for us."

"Yes, yes, indeed! I have hired some *renowned* actors to perform a magnificent play, though I shall not tell you what it is for fear that I shall spoil the performance!" Lord Dunford, seemingly quite pleased that he had managed to convince Henry to return to the soiree, rubbed his hands together. "If there is anything that you require, however, you must inform me of it. I will do whatever you wish."

Henry shook his head but smiled with it. "Not at all, Lord Dunford. There is nothing that I require, though I thank you for your gracious consideration. You are an excellent host."

This made Lord Dunford flush, and he quickly thanked Henry before leading him from the library, snapping his fingers so that the footman nearby came quickly to offer Henry a drink. Taking one, Henry nodded his thanks and, after a moment, quickly stepped away. Meandering through the crowd, he smiled briefly at one or two acquaintances as he made his way to the drawing room, aware of the delight that flashed through many an expression at his presence. He looked away from every young lady as quickly as he could, though he knew he could not avoid them forever.

"You have decided to rejoin us all, I see." Lord Kendall stepped forward and, snagging Henry's attention, offered a wry smile. "You found the many exclamations of delight at your arrival to be a little too much?"

"As you might have expected," Henry muttered, taking a sip of his whisky before stepping back towards the wall of the drawing room. "You know very well that I have been a little... troubled of late."

"Because you have not been able to find any young lady who can meet every single one of your expectations."

Henry took another sip of his drink. "Indeed."

"Then I – "

"Good evening, Your Grace! How delightful to see you again."

Henry let out a small, inward sigh before turning fully to greet a lady that he could not recall. "Good evening." He inclined his head, just as Lord Kendall did the same. "I do hope you are enjoying the soiree? I hear that Lord Dunford has an *excellent* play for us this evening." It was not the first time in these last two weeks that Henry had been unable to remember a lady's face or title, but he had now become quite accustomed to being able to continue a conversation without requiring the need to do so. There were too many faces, too many names, and too many 'how wonderful, Your Grace', for him to be clear about who was who.

"Yes, it has been wonderful thus far. Now," the lady continued, fluttering her fingers at him as though he were a bird she wished to catch, "I do hope that you will permit me to introduce you to my daughter? We did try to do so before but she was stolen away by another gentleman for one of the dances that evening. And when she returned, you had yourself stepped away to dance!"

A sudden tension flashed through Henry and he scowled, though quickly fought to take that out of his expression. He instantly recalled who it was that he was speaking with, remembered that it was none other than Lady Hampshire and her most disagreeable daughter – the one who had stepped away from him without permitting Lady Newton to make the formal introductions.

"Your Grace?" Lady Hampshire blinked, concern in her voice. "Is there something wrong? I do hope I have not said something wrong. I was only asking for an introduction to my daughter, though I am quite sure that you have had a good many introductions this evening alone!"

Lord Kendall chuckled, breaking the strain between Henry and Lady Hampshire. "You are quite right there, Lady Hampshire. Though I am sure another introduction will not do any harm?" He shot a sharp look towards Henry, pulling him out of his own irritation and forcing him to respond in as amiable manner as he could manage. Propriety demanded that he not only smile but nod, seeing the relief that swept into Lady Hampshire's expression as he did so. "Yes, of course. I would be very glad to become acquainted with your daughter."

"Oh, how wonderful. Thank you, Your Grace. Do excuse me for a moment, I shall return presently."

Henry watched as Lady Hampshire scurried across the room, ignoring the sharp look that Lord Kendall was sending him, one that he could practically feel pressing into him. He knew very well that his irritation with the as yet unintroduced young lady was still very much present but he was also keenly aware that he could not permit such a thing to come out in either his expression or his manner.

"Thank you for waiting, Your Grace." Lady Hampshire beamed at him, though the young lady in question did not appear to be in the least bit delighted in being present, given that she did not smile nor even raise her gaze to his. Instead, she was looking away, her lips a little flattened as she waited for her mother to make the introductions.

"Your Grace – and Lord Kendall also, of course – might I present my daughter? This is Lydia, my *only* daughter who has only just made her come out!" She gestured to Henry as slowly, the young lady turned her gaze towards him. "Lydia, this is the Duke of Melrose and his close friend, the Marquess of Kendall."

To her credit, the young lady curtsied beautifully, speaking just she ought though there was no hint of happiness in her voice. "Good evening, Your Grace. Good evening, Lord Kendall. It is a delight to be introduced to you both."

Henry inclined his head, though Lord Kendall swept into a proper bow, shaming him just a little given that he had not done such a thing. Catching the slight lift of the lady's eyebrows, Henry cleared his throat and looked away from her, a little embarrassed and then, thereafter, frustrated at his embarrassment. "I hope that you find the soiree a pleasant one, Lady Lydia." There was not any sort of desire within him to begin any sort of conversation, disliking that she showed no eagerness to be in his company. He turned his head to the left, wondering if he would be able to see someone else eager to catch his attention by which he might be able to make an excuse for stepping away.

"Might I ask if you are the only child?" Lord Kendall asked, making Henry scowl at him in irritation. "Your father is the Earl of Hampshire, is that not correct? I am sure that I am acquainted with your brother, though I might be mistaken?"

"You are quite correct, Lord Kendall." The warmth in Lady Lydia's voice made Henry's scowl darken, noting how Lady Hampshire had stepped back just a little, now engaging herself in further conversation with another acquaintance, though her gaze glanced back towards her daughter now and again. Clearly, she was determined to permit her daughter as much conversation with Lord Kendall and Henry as she could.

"Then your brother is Lord Gillingham?"

The smile that spread across Lady Lydia's face as she nodded in answer to Lord Kendall's question made Henry's heart lurch for just a moment. There was something about that smile – evidently genuine – that sent a flush of color into her cheeks, making her green eyes sparkle as her red curls danced. At that moment, Henry was struck by the beauty of the young lady in front of him, seeing now that there was a pleasantness to her though it was not, at this juncture, being directed towards him.

"I am well acquainted with Lord Gillingham!" Lord Kendall exclaimed, beaming back at Lady Lydia. "We were at Eton together! He is wed and settled now, is he not?"

"Yes, he is. Though I do miss him a great deal." Lady Lydia's smile softened. "He and I were very close as children, and he was always encouraging of my pursuits and desires."

"How very pleasant for you," Lord Kendall remarked, throwing a glance towards Henry; a glance which suggested that he try to involve himself in the conversation in some way. "And what sort of pursuits do you enjoy?"

Lady Lydia's smile returned with a new strength. "Oh, I

am afraid that it is not in the least bit anything that a young lady *ought* to do, Lord Kendall. In fact, my mother has forbade me to speak of my hobbies for fear that it shall startle and upset many a gentleman."

Henry snorted at this, rolling his eyes at her. "My dear lady, I am sure that unless your pursuits involve hunting, shooting and other interests kept only for gentlemen, we shall not be in the least bit astonished." He chuckled, imagining that her interests were something akin to pursuing an instrument other than the pianoforte or the harp, or mayhap enjoying taking a hold of the reins when she and her brother took a drive together. It could surely be nothing horrifying!

"Is that so?" Lady Lydia's smile had crumpled, her eyes sharp as she turned her attention towards him. "Might I ask what it is that you would consider to be *gentlemen's* pursuits, Your Grace? Things that young ladies ought not to do?"

For whatever reason, Henry felt as though he was about to walk into a trap – a trap set by his own words – but he certainly could not let himself refuse to answer. He had to defend his thoughts, had to state quite clearly what he believed for to refuse to do so would give her the impression that he had no answer and he could not permit that! He shrugged, aware of the warning look that Lord Kendall sent him but choosing to ignore it.

"Well, Lady Lydia, I do not think that a young lady ought to ride astride, for example."

"Though you think they should still be able to ride, I presume?" Her eyebrow arched. "So that in itself is not a pursuit saved only for gentlemen."

Henry hesitated, aware that his dislike of this particular young lady was returning in even greater strength than before. "Indeed."

"Then what pursuits, might I ask, do you consider only to be for a gentleman?"

A burst of heat in his chest sent fire up into his neck and face. She was asking him pertinent questions, yes, but that in itself was a frustration for him. Should not a young lady seek only to listen to his thoughts and accept them instead of questioning them in this manner?

"Aha, I think you might have befuddled him, Lady Lydia!"

His irritation growing fiercely, Henry threw an angry look toward Lord Kendall, but his friend only grinned at him, clearly not in the least bit interested in Henry's upset.

"Not in the least," he answered, smartly. "Lady Lydia, I think that young ladies ought not to drink port, for there is plenty of other things that they might partake of, should they wish it."

Much to his surprise, she giggled, her eyes twinkling, just as Lord Kendall let out a guffaw.

"But, Your Grace, I should hardly call drinking the occasional glass of port to be a pursuit or a hobby. You specifically spoke of pursuits and it is that which I have questioned."

Henry drew himself up, the fire in his chest now engulfing him. "They should not do anything that a gentleman does, such as hunting or shooting. They should not play cards – " He stopped short, rubbing one hand over his face, realizing that he had misspoken again. "That is to say, they should not *gamble* at cards, in my opinion, though I am aware that some do. Only in very small amounts, I am sure." Seeing the smile beginning to curve up Lady Lydia's face, he looked away from her, feeling as though every part of him was burning. "They ought not to drive a carriage, a curricle, a phaeton, or any other such thing. As I have said,

Lady Lydia, ladies such as yourself ought not to pursue anything that is reserved for gentlemen, they should only consider those hobbies which have already been considered suitable for them."

Her eyebrows fell a little heavier over her eyes. "Reading, then? Is that to be suitable?"

"Reading, of course. Though not to a great extent and exclusively to novels and the like."

"So you do not think ladies of the *ton* should pursue any sort of learning?" She threw up her hands, her eyes a trifle narrowed now. "A governess must be considered a great waste of time and money, then!"

Seeing that she had bested him again, Henry ran one hand over his face, aware that he ought to step away from her but feeling as though, if he did, he would be seen as a fool in her eyes and mayhap even in the eyes of Lord Kendall. "A governess is not a waste of time, though a young lady need not be educated in any way beyond what a governess teaches."

Lady Lydia sniffed, turning her gaze away. "You hold, then, that any further learning beyond what a lady is given during her upbringing is considered improper?"

"And entirely unnecessary," he added, firmly. "A bluestocking is a shame to society and her family, Lady Lydia, and ought to be spurned. As would be a young lady seeking to go out hunting with the gentlemen of the *ton* or who chose to ride astride rather than sidesaddle!" He held her gaze, lifting his chin when her eyes grew cold.

"I would have thought that a Duke, with all his fine education, would have recognized the blessing that such a thing brought him." Lady Lydia took a small step closer to him, her eyes holding his now with such an intensity, he could not seem to look away. "And I would have expected that a Duke would have lacked this sharp, determined judgment that appears to state that *his* opinion is the correct one. Does not your education teach you that there are differing viewpoints and different experiences to be considered?"

"I... " Henry did not know what to say but nor could he pull his gaze away from her. Lady Lydia was pushing him into a conversation he did not want to have, into thoughts and considerations that made him feel very uncomfortable indeed.

"Come, Lydia. I think you have spoken with the Duke and Lord Kendall long enough."

It was Lady Hampshire who interrupted their conversation, putting one hand on her daughter's arm and forcing Lady Lydia's attention to be pulled away from Henry. "Thank you for your time in speaking with my daughter, Your Grace. And to you also, Lord Kendall. I hear that you are already acquainted with my son?"

Lord Kendall nodded and smiled, though Henry continued to glower. "I am. Your son and I still write to each other on occasion and I shall remember to do so again very soon, so I might inform him that I have had the delightful pleasure of being introduced to his sister." He inclined his head as Lady Hampshire smiled, though Henry was sure there was a tightness in her expression that had not been there before.

"You are very kind, Lord Kendall."

"Not at all. I do hope that you and I might speak again, Lady Lydia? Mayhap we shall see one another at a ball one evening?"

This took some of the tension from Lady Hampshire's expression as Lady Lydia nodded and smiled, though she had turned herself bodily away from Henry and instead, set her attention to Lord Kendall. "Yes, I should be glad to continue our conversation at another time, Lord Kendall. Good evening." She offered Henry a cursory glance, though the corner of her mouth lifted slightly in a moue of distaste. "And to you also, Your Grace."

"Lady Lydia." Henry inclined his head, filled with both relief at her departure and a seeming lingering dislike of the young lady as she moved away from him. He saw how Lady Hampshire's head tilted towards her daughter, clearly saying something though quite what it would be, he did not know.

"Well, you made a very firm impression upon her, I must say!" Lord Kendall chuckled as Henry scowled, his laugh made all the worse by the way he slapped Henry on the shoulder as he did so. "Goodness, are you truly so fervent about what a young lady ought not to pursue?"

"I most certainly am." Henry drew himself up, his chin forward. "I think that to have a bluestocking in one's family but be a very great shame indeed."

Lord Kendall rolled his eyes. "It should not surprise me, I suppose. Given your list of requirements – a list which, I know, has not yet found even one young lady to fulfill it – it should not be as astonishing to me that you have such firm opinions."

Henry turned to his friend sharply. "You cannot tell me that you would be contented with a wife who went out hunting or the like?"

Lord Kendall hesitated, then shrugged. "I think that if I fall in love with a young lady, I should find such a thing yet another part of her character to love," he answered, as Henry snorted in ridicule. "A young lady does not need to fit all that I desire to make me a suitable wife, I do not think. Besides, think what fun it would be to go out riding with one's wife, only to find that she is a better rider than you!"

Henry shook his head. "No. I will not even imagine such a dreadful thing. A young lady, the one who will be mistress of my home, will do all that is expected of her and that shall be the extent of it. I shall not have someone who has stepped outside of the realms of propriety for even a *moment*! No, whoever I marry will be all that I require her to be and nothing more." He shivered at the thought of what it might be like to wed a bluestocking, his lip curling as he realized, no doubt, that Lady Lydia herself was one such creature given her defense of the notion.

It does not matter, he told himself, turning around entirely so that he did not have to look in the same direction as Lady Lydia. *I do not think that I shall be in company with Lady Lydia again this Season, and that shall suit me very well indeed.*

CHAPTER FOUR

"Lydia?"

Lydia's heart slammed hard against her ribs as she quickly rose from her chair, setting the book down on the seat behind her before sitting back down again. Then, with haste in every movement, she reached for her embroidery – a piece that she had been working on for some months now and had made very little progress with. Not that her mother would notice, however.

"Ah, here you are." Lady Hampshire stepped into the drawing room though her eyes quickly darted all around Lydia rather than looking directly into her face. "What are you doing?"

Lydia held up her embroidery, aware that her mother's sharp gaze was solely because of her fear that Lydia had been reading again. "This."

"I see." There was no sense of trust in Lady Hampshire's voice, only doubt but Lydia did not care. Yes, her seat was now a little uncomfortable because of the book she now sat on but she had no intention of shifting to her feet, no matter how long she had to sit there!

"I wanted to speak with you about your conversation with Lord Kendall and the Duke of Melrose last evening." Lady Hampshire did not sit down but remained on her feet, a slight frown flickering across her forehead. "Though you seem to have done well with the Marquess of Kendall, it was clear that you had upset the Duke in some way. You refused to tell me what it was you said to him last evening and I must hope that now, you will choose to do so."

Lydia hid her scowl as best she could. Her mother had spoken a little harshly to her the previous evening, demanding to know what it was she had said that had made the Duke of Melrose scowl at her but Lydia had refused to entertain an answer. Instead, she had simply shrugged lightly and said that the Duke had appeared to be in something of an irritable mood since the very moment she had been introduced. This had not satisfied her mother, though she had appeared to agree with Lydia's assessment of the Duke's state of mind.

"Lydia?"

Seeing that her silence would not be a satisfactory answer, Lydia looked down at her embroidery, feigning an interest in it. "As I have said, Mama, the Duke of Melrose did seem to be very unhappy with being present at the soiree. I think he might have been a little jealous at Lord Kendall's connection to my brother."

"I beg your pardon?" Lady Hampshire let out a laugh that was both cold and harsh. "You cannot expect me to believe that the Duke of Melrose was jealous of his friend's conversation with you!"

Lydia looked back at her mother. "That was only a thought, Mama," she answered, ignoring the small stab of pain that lanced her heart. "Lord Kendall was, as you saw for yourself, very eager indeed to be in conversation with me and has hopes to dance with me! Surely, if I had said something to upset the Duke of Melrose, Lord Kendall would have had the same expression as he! There would have been *two* upset gentlemen, rather than one."

Lady Hampshire frowned heavily, clearly not fully assured by Lydia's response. "If I find out that you said something about your desire to further your learning and understanding, then I will be *greatly* displeased, Lydia. I am sure that –"

A knock at the door had Lady Hampshire's warnings fall silent and she quickly called for the servant to enter. A footman came in, handing Lady Hampshire a card, though she quickly looked towards Lydia.

"Are you expecting Lady Markham this afternoon?"

"Yes, I am!" Lydia set aside her embroidery immediately, making to rise to her feet only to recall the book she had underneath her. "Might she join us, Mama?"

Lady Hampshire sighed heavily. "Lydia, I am not quite finished with my conversation with you but... " She sighed again. "On this occasion, I shall leave you and your friend to take tea."

"Thank you, Mama."

With a nod, Lady Hampshire made to leave the room, only to glance back at Lydia and frown. "Are you so improper that you will not rise to greet your friend in the correct way?"

"I shall, of course." Lydia forced a smile, praying that her mother would not linger and wait to make certain that she did so, relieved when, with a click of her tongue to make clear her disapproval, Lady Hampshire walked out of the door.

Relieved, Lydia got to her feet, turning to pick up the book but managing, somehow, to tangle it up in her skirts all the same. Frustrated, she began to mutter to herself, only to hear a peal of laughter coming from the other side of the room.

"Whatever are you doing, Lydia?"

With a wry smile, Lydia turned to face her friend, only for the book to drop to the floor, the thump making Sophie's eyebrows lift. "Good afternoon, Sophie," Lydia began, turning around again in an attempt to find the book and, seeing it, bending to pluck it from the floor. "Aha! I have you now."

"Were you reading?" Coming to sit down, Sophie gave Lydia a slightly confused look. "I do not understand why you were so tangled in your skirts!"

Lydia laughed and handed the book to her friend before going to ring the bell for a tea tray. "I was, yes. But when I heard my mother coming, I quickly sat on the book and it was only when she left that I was able to find it again."

Sophie laughed again just as Lydia sat down, the rueful smile still on her face. "Goodness, that must have been a little difficult for you!"

"It was certainly uncomfortable."

Her friend tipped her head just a little. "I am sorry that you cannot be encouraged in what you love."

Lydia let out a slow breath, lifting her shoulders as she did so. "I cannot change it, I suppose. So there is nothing to be done aside from attempting to hide my love of it from my parents." Her lips quirked. "Though I did not do so when it came to speaking with the Duke of Melrose and the Marquess of Kendall last evening. Goodness, is not the Duke of Melrose an arrogant gentleman?"

Her friend spread out her hands. "I could not say. I am not acquainted with him particularly well, though my husband knows him better than I. But is it not expected for a Duke to be arrogant? I would have thought that it would not be a surprise to learn of his condescension."

"I suppose that is true. Though, as I have said, I did make it quite clear that my respect for his opinion was somewhat lacking." Wincing as she recalled the heavy frown that had pulled at the Duke's forehead, she shook her head. "I must hope that he does not say anything to either my mother or my father."

Sophie looked back at her steadily. "What did you say?"

"Not too much," Lydia answered, still having a vague sense of triumph lingering in her from the previous evening's conversation. "He stated quite clearly that young ladies ought not to do various things, that it would be wrong or shameful for them to be learned and knowledgeable beyond that of what a governess teaches."

"Ah." Sophie rolled her eyes. "I am sure you made your feelings on that subject more than clear."

"I certainly did."

"Then I think that very good," her friend declared, determinedly. "And that is one of the reasons I am come to call on you today."

Lydia's eyebrows lifted. "Oh?"

"I have some connections to The London Chronicle," Sophie continued, with a wave of her hand. "They are always looking for something new and interesting to place within it. I did wonder whether or not you might wish to approach them about writing a piece or two?"

The idea did quickly pique Lydia's interest, though doubts instantly began to cloud her mind. "I do not know if I am much good at writing and, even if I were to be, whatever should I write about?"

"You are quite excellent at the written word," came her friend's reply, as the tea tray was brought in. "I have had some thoughts on what you could write within it. Though I know that you love all manner of learning and you know a good many things, not everything will be of interest to the *ton* and therefore, rejected by The London Chronicle."

Lydia's lips pulled to one side as she thought, the idea taking a greater hold of her mind.

"You might be able to suggest that you write a brief history of England?" Sophie continued, shrugging her shoulders. "Or different parts of England, mayhap?"

Getting to her feet to pour the tea, Lydia considered the idea. "Perhaps the traditions and customs of each place?"

"Precisely!"

"Though that might not capture the interest of many, only those who live in that particular area," Lydia muttered, pouring the tea carefully. It was only when she set it down that she was hit with another thought, one that made her pause.

"What is it?" Evidently aware that Lydia had thought of something, Sophie leaned forward in her chair, her eyes rounded. "What are you thinking?"

"What if I wrote about the history of a place and connected it to a family here in London now?" Lydia's heart quickened. "I would be able to study, to read, and to explore as much as I wished! Then I would be able to take what I have learned and present it in an article! Would that not get the attention of the *ton*?"

Her friend began to nod slowly, a smile beginning to spread across her face. "Indeed, I think it would! It would mean that the family of whoever you chose to write about would be interested, but there would also be a curiosity from the *ton* about whatever history you choose to divulge. It could be something between learning and gossip!"

"Precisely!"

"Though," Sophie added, holding up one hand, palm out towards Lydia, "you may have to use a different name."

Lydia's shoulders slumped, though she quickly understood what it was her friend meant. "You think that The London Chronicle would not accept articles from a lady."

At this, Sophie shook her head. "No, it is not that. The London Chronicle already has many a lady's name attached to it! I worry that your parents would be greatly displeased and prevent you from doing anything more than one article! And what would you do then?" She shrugged. "Besides which, what if the person or family you choose to write about is displeased by your attentions? You need to protect yourself."

With her understanding clear now, Lydia nodded but smiled all the same. "I think that is quite a wonderful suggestion! I am delighted with your idea, Sophie. Thank you for thinking of me."

"But of course." Her friend reached to pick up her tea cup. "I know that you have struggled against your parents' disapproval for some time and that even now, it must be very difficult indeed."

"It is made easier when I have your friendship and understanding," Lydia answered, feeling herself happier than she had been in some time. "Thank you again, Sophie. This is quite wonderful!"

Taking a sip of her tea and then reaching for one of the small cakes that had been set out, Sophie shot Lydia a quick look. "I must ask, who will you write about first?"

Only one name came to mind and Lydia chuckled softly, sitting back in her chair and grinning at her friend. "Well, I must get the attention of the *ton*, must I not?"

"Yes, you must."

"And I must write something to intrigue and delight, yes?"

Sophie nodded.

"Then I think I shall write about the Duke of Melrose," Lydia said, with a chuckle as Sophie gasped. "And mayhap, if I am fortunate, it will bring down that arrogance *just* a little." Her smile faded. "Though it also might do precisely the opposite also."

Sophie tipped her head, her eyes going towards the window for a few moments as she thought. Then, with a small nod, she directed her gaze back towards Lydia. "I think that an excellent idea, however."

"You do?"

"I do."

Lydia took in a deep breath and then set her shoulders. "Then I shall do all I can to learn about the Duke of Melrose and write an article that will, I hope, do all that I want it do to. I can only hope that it will be accepted by The London Chronicle!"

"As do I," came the reply. "But you write well and I am sure this will be an excellent thing for you."

Lydia nodded and reached for her own tea, a sense of excitement building in her, something she had not felt in some time. Now, finally, she had a chance to pursue her love of learning but this time, with a purpose.

She could only pray others liked what she wrote, otherwise it would be only one article and nothing thereafter. And then what would there be in London for her?

CHAPTER FIVE

"Are you quite ready to give up yet?"

Henry glanced to Lord Kendall, then shook his head. "If you are asking me what I think you are asking, then the answer is no."

Lord Kendall chuckled. "I am asking you whether or not you are ready to admit that your list of requirements is much too long and will never be entirely fulfilled."

"Then the answer is *certainly* no." Henry chuckled wryly as his friend rolled his eyes. "There are many young ladies in London and I have not been introduced to all of them as yet. And those I *have* been introduced to, I do not know."

"And this is how you intend to get to know some of them, is it? Standing alone, in amongst a small group of trees while the rest of the *ton* make their way through Hyde Park?"

A trifle irritated at his friend's sarcasm, Henry let it wash over him. "I am only observing the young ladies present at the moment." He nodded his head in the direction of one gentleman standing with another lady. "I can see my uncle, in fact. I did not know he was in London and I must, of course, go to speak with him."

"Your uncle?" Lord Kendall followed the direction of Henry's gaze, then nodded. "Ah, Lord Chesterfield. He is an Earl, is he not?"

"He is. I have not spoken with him in some time. I shall certainly have to speak with him this afternoon. But, I do not yet want to make my way down into the crowd until I have seen who *else* is present. The debutantes in particular, you understand."

Lord Kendall snorted. "It is the fashionable hour, there is barely going to be grass left to stand on soon enough! You must decide who it is that you wish to speak to and, thereafter, go to do so without hesitation. Otherwise every face will become blurred and you will lose any awareness of who you have spoken to and who you have not."

A trifle confused, Henry looked to his friend. "I do not know what you mean."

Lord Kendall flung out one hand towards the slowly increasing crowd. "I mean to say that there are so *many* young ladies here, you shall find yourself surrounded! Despite your intentions to speak to only this young lady or that young lady, you will be so overwhelmed that you will be quite overcome."

Henry frowned. "So what should I do?"

"You should decide on one or two young ladies that you intend to improve your connection with and, thereafter, go to do so. Once you decide that they do not bring you all that you desire, then you choose another young lady to replace the first and so on and so forth." Lord Kendall's eyes glinted as he attempted to hide a smile. "And then, once you have made your way through every single young lady in London, you shall admit to me that you were entirely unsuccessful, that your list of requirements was quite ridiculous and you shall beg me for guidance and advice. Which, of course, I shall be glad to give."

"Is that so?" Henry chuckled as his friend grinned and nodded. He considered for a few minutes, slowly coming to accept that his friend was quite correct in his suggestion that he choose only a few young ladies to consider, rather than looking through the crowd and wondering who he ought to speak with on this one occasion or who else he might be introduced to. "Very well, you are right, I suppose."

"I am?" Lord Kendall's eyes widened only for him to laugh. "Greater words have never been spoken!"

Ignoring this, Henry shook his head. "Might you come down from your lofty position and be able to tell me who it is that you think I ought to improve my acquaintance with first?"

The smile left Lord Kendall's face as he considered this, looking around at the crowd near them. Then, he nudged Henry, his eyes fixed straight ahead.

"There, that is Lady Judith, daughter to the Marquess of Kent. You have been introduced to her, yes?"

Henry frowned. "Is it the young lady with the feathers in her bonnet?"

"Yes."

"Then yes, I have. Though I do not recall any sort of conversation that came thereafter."

Lord Kendall nodded, seemingly satisfied at this. "Then she is one. And what about Lady Ann? Her brother has recently taken on the title from his late father, the Earl of Gateshead."

"Very well." Henry recognized the second young lady at once, recalling how her laugh had sent a shiver down his spine. "Though Lady Ann did laugh a little too sharply for me and – "

"And she might have been very nervous when it came to speaking with a Duke and you will not base your consideration of a young lady on whether her laugh pleases you or not." Lord Kendall frowned heavily, though Henry was sure there was a smile still lurking there. "That was not one of your requirements, I am sure."

"Then it should have been," Henry muttered, as a choked exclamation came from his friend. "Come then, join me, if you would."

Lord Kendall shook his head. "No, indeed not. I have my own bride to find, recall?"

Henry chuckled, a question lifting his eyebrows. "And given that you are so determined I shall fail in my endeavors, what is to say that you will not find delight and compatibility where I do not?"

This gave Lord Kendall pause. "Ah. Yes. You might find Lady Ann's laugh displeasing but I might find it delightful."

"Precisely."

Lord Kendall grinned as he spread out one hand towards the ladies near to them. "Then of course, I shall join you. Please, Your Grace, lead the way."

With a roll of his eyes and a wry smile on his lips, Henry marched past Lord Kendall and made his way directly towards the young lady with feathers in her bonnet, pausing only to shake his uncle's hand with a promise that he would return to speak at length with him very soon. He did not think much of the feathers, finding them a little too *red* and ostentatious, given that she was a debutante and meant to only be wearing light colors given her standing. Though, he reminded himself, that directive was not in his list of requirements either.

"Lord Kent," Henry muttered, inclining his head as he came closer to the gentleman. "Good afternoon."

"Your Grace!" The gentleman's eyebrows lifted though he bowed quickly, seeming to be surprised that Henry had come to speak with him. "Good afternoon."

"You are acquainted with the Marquess of Kendall, yes?" Henry gestured to Lord Kendall, who was already smiling at Lady Judith and, much to Henry's irritation, Lady Judith was blushing gently at the gentleman's attentions. Clearly, Lord Kendall was not going to make it easy for Henry to seek out whether or not a lady would be suitable for him! Perhaps it had been a mistake to ask him to join the conversation.

"Yes, yes, very well acquainted." Lord Kent gestured to his daughter. "You know Lady Judith, I think?"

Henry looked to the lady and inclined his head, seeing the color rise in her cheeks and feeling himself a little more satisfied that she was now considering *him* rather than Lord Kendall. "Yes, we were introduced at a ball, I think."

The color began to fade from her face. "Forgive me for correcting you, Your Gracee, but it was Lord Harlow's dinner."

"Ah. Yes, of course." Henry coughed quietly, a little embarrassed to have made such a mistake. "And tell me, Lady Judith, do you like those feathers in your bonnet?" It was not a question he had meant to ask but given his embarrassment at making a mistake, it had come to his lips without warning.

Lady Judith blinked.

"*I* think they are quite lovely," Lord Kendall said hastily, shooting Henry a glance that was filled with both confusion and frustration. "Is it something that you had purposely made?"

"I – I chose the feathers, yes." Lady Judith glanced from Henry to Lord Kendall and back again. "And the ribbon, of course. The pink is to complement them."

Her eyes darted again from Lord Kendall to Henry but Henry, not sure what he ought to say only looked away.

"Which it does beautifully." Again, Lord Kendall spoke, seeming to reassure Lady Judith though Henry did not quite understand as to why this was necessary. All he had been trying to do was understand if Lady Judith had picked these feathers herself and, if she had, what her thoughts had been in the process. That was all.

"Are you in London for the entire Season, Your Grace?" Lord Kent wanted to know, pulling Henry's thoughts away from Lady Judith and her feathers. "I hope you have found it a pleasant experience so far."

"On the whole, it has been enjoyable, yes." Henry sniffed and looked back at Lady Judith, considering her. She was beautiful, with her blue eyes and fair hair, gently pouting lips and pale complexion but that did not mean that she would satisfy all that he desired in a wife. "I do hope that I will be permitted to come to take tea with you one day soon, Lady Judith?"

This seemed to astonish Lady Judith a great deal, for she stared at him with wide eyes for some moments, her mouth a little ajar – and that made Henry frown. He could not have a young lady by his side who would be so overwhelmed by whatever circumstances came to her!

"Judith?" Lord Kent set a hand on his daughter's arm. "His Grace was asking you if he could come to take tea?"

Lady Judith blinked quickly. "I – I did not mean to hesitate, Your Grace. In all truth, you astonish me by your consideration and I feel honoured by your request. Yes, of course, you would be welcome to call at any time preferable to you."

This buoyed Henry's spirits a little, seeing that Lady Judith's reaction to his request came from a clear surprise, perhaps recognizing his standing and considering herself in light of that. Such a thing pleased him, he had to admit, so with that in mind, he gave her a nod.

"Excellent. I hope to call later this week." After a few more moments of conversation, Henry excused himself and stepped away, leaving Lord Kendall to the conversation. He made his way directly towards Lady Ann, though he then began to slow his steps, recognizing that he was not acquainted with her as yet.

He frowned. Should he wait for Lord Kendall? To do so would mean that he would be drawn into conversation with others and might then miss his opportunity to speak with Lady Ann, would it not?

"Your Grace, good afternoon!"

Henry sighed inwardly, recognizing that his hesitation had led him into the very situation he had not wanted to be in. "Good afternoon, Lady Hampshire. Lord Hampshire, I presume?" Being quickly introduced to the Earl, Henry let his gaze fall to Lady Lydia who, he noticed, was regarding him with a flicker of something – perhaps interest – in her eye. It was a rather strange feeling to be studied so, for she was not looking at him in the way that other young ladies did. There was no flush of heat in her cheeks, no sparkle in her eyes, no demure lowering of her lashes as she smiled gently. Rather, it was with consideration that she gazed at him, as though she were trying to make him out, trying to understand him without a word being exchanged between them.

He did not much like it.

"I hear that you are already acquainted with my daughter and that your friend is acquainted with my son!" Lord Hampshire beamed, pleased that there was a connection of sorts between them. "Is Lord Kendall here this afternoon?"

Henry nodded. "Yes, he is." He caught the way Lord Hampshire threw a glance at his daughter and let his eyebrows lift in surprise. Did Lord Hampshire think that Lady Lydia might have a chance of catching Lord Kendall's interest? That made his stomach twist at the thought, for if that were to occur, would it not damage his friendship with Lord Kendall? He could not very well pretend he liked Lady Lydia and Lord Kendall was already well aware of that.

"He will come to join me soon," Henry told him, being careful to keep his gaze away from Lady Lydia, though the way she continued to watch him made his skin crawl with uncomfortable displeasure. "He is to introduce me to Lady Ann, daughter to Lord Gateshead."

"Oh, but Lydia could do such a thing if you required it!" Lord Hampshire continued to smile broadly in Henry's direction, gesturing to his daughter as he did so. "She and Lady Ann have only just finished in conversation and I know she would be *delighted* to make an introduction. Would you not, Lydia?"

Was it just Henry's imagination or did he hear a sigh escape from Lady Lydia's mouth?

"If you should like me to introduce you, then I would be glad too, of course." Lady Lydia spoke in a dull tone, without a single smile crossing her lips. "She is just a little way over here."

"And she can take you to Lady Ann, of course." Lady Hampshire slipped her arm through her husband's. "It is only a few steps away so we need not join you." She turned her attention to her daughter, a thin smile on her face. "On you go now, Lydia. Make sure the Duke is properly introduced to Lady Ann."

Henry frowned, opening his mouth to say that there was no need for such a thing, only to see Lady Lydia turn on her heel and make to walk away from him. There was no chance for him to refuse now, no opportunity for him to say that no, he did not need her assistance. With another glance towards the Earl and Countess – Lady Hampshire with her small smile still present and Lord Hampshire with a wide smile on his round face – Henry nodded and, heaviness in every step, followed after Lady Lydia.

He came beside her, seeing her glance up at him only to then look away again. They walked in silence for a few minutes as frustration began to climb up Henry's spine.

"I thought you said she was only a few steps away."

"I think, Your Grace, you will find that the statement came from my mother." Lady Lydia sniffed and looked up at him again. "It will only be a few more minutes."

Henry's jaw tightened, a little frustrated that Lord and Lady Hampshire had, in their own way, determined to place himself and their daughter together. "I did not think that we would be walking together, Lady Lydia." He could not quite keep the frustration out of his voice and caught the sharp look she sent him, seeing the hint of red in her cheeks.

"Your Grace, I am well aware that you do not wish to be in my company but be assured that I feel the very same. I have no desire to be in company with you for any longer than I must and am doing this only because my mother and father made it impossible for me to refuse."

Her clear way of speaking and her somewhat sharp tone made Henry's eyebrows lift, utterly astonished that a young lady of quality would speak so to him. "Is that so?" Doubt flooded through his tone, his head held high as he inwardly set aside all that she had said, not certain he believed her. Despite her clear disinclination towards his company, surely she still took some pleasure in being seen in his company?

As though she had heard his thoughts, Lady Lydia responded quickly. "No doubt you will wonder why a young lady such as myself is not delighted to be in your company, given that you are a Duke," she began, the edge of her lip curling. "However, you will find that I am a young lady who is *not* inclined to lose her head simply because she is company with a Duke."

"I can see that." The words tumbled out of Henry's mouth before he could prevent them, her sharp tone and blunt remarks injuring him in a way he could not quite understand. "Though mayhap you ought to consider a little more just who it is that you are in company with?"

This did not bring the expected response for Lady Lydia did not glance up at him with worry in her eyes, did not look back at him with any sort of concern. Instead, he heard her make a quiet exclamation, something between a snort and a laugh.

That made his face heat, the blood in his veins beginning to burn.

"You are unlike any young lady I have ever met," he told her, brusquely. "I think your mother and father ought to be ashamed of your behavior."

"Oh, they already are, Your Grace," came the reply, a lightness in her tone that did not speak of any sort of upset. "You may well have ascertained this by now, but I am, completely and utterly, a bluestocking. I love all manner of learning, I find it deeply fascinating to discover new things and I am certainly *not* going to be bound by what society expects of me. So yes, you may well state that my parents ought to be ashamed of my behavior but the truth is, Your Grace, there is nothing but frustration and upset at my decision to pursue such interests. So I do not think that my dislike of being in a Duke's company will cause them any great upset, for they have a good deal of that already."

Henry did not know what to say, finding himself caught between something like shame at how he had spoken and a lingering irritation that nothing he had said had, in any way, affected Lady Lydia. He did not have the opportunity to respond further, however, for the lady drew close to a small group of gentlemen and ladies, and within moments, Henry found himself introduced not only to Lady Ann but to one or two others that he was not acquainted with.

"A pleasant day, is it not, Your Grace?" Lady Ann spoke gently and with a warm smile on her lips but Henry did not find his heart or mind pulled towards her in any way. Instead, he found himself considering Lady Lydia all the more, his thoughts still stirred up over all she had said and revealed to him.

"A fine day, yes." Managing to stumble over his words, Henry cleared his throat and forced a smile, looking around the small group and trying to push all thoughts of Lady Lydia from himself. "Though it is quite busy, is it not?"

This sent a murmur of acknowledgment around the group and, much to Henry's relief, pulled the conversation from him. He was able to take a few moments to regain his sense of composure, glancing this way and that to ascertain where Lady Lydia was... only to realize that she was gone.

No sense of relief filled him. Instead, his brows pulled together in a heavy frown as he considered all that she had said to him, struggling to understand why his own thoughts still lingered on the lady.

Remember what Lord Kendall told you, he reminded himself. *One or two ladies at a time. That means I do not need to concentrate on anyone other than Lady Ann and Lady Judith for the time being.* The edge of his mouth crept upwards. *And it is not as though I would ever consider Lady Lydia!* With that planted firmly in his mind, Henry lifted his chin, took a breath, and reentered the conversation with a fresh confidence and determination within him, quite certain that, in time, he would be able to fully forget Lady Lydia entirely.

CHAPTER SIX

I do not want to cry.
Despite her determination not to do so, Lydia felt the press of tears in her eyes as she walked away from the Duke of Melrose. Whether he realized it or not, his words had been harsh and injurious, though she had pretended that they meant nothing to her.

Stopping for a moment, Lydia looked down at the grass at her feet as though she found them peculiarly interesting, all the while taking in long, steadying breaths to calm herself. She had spoken much too freely and with too much of a blunt manner, she realized, and that in itself had been foolish. Though all the same, she did not deserve the Duke's harshness, surely?

"Lydia?"

Lifting her head, Lydia almost melted with relief at the sight of Lady Markham. "Sophie. Thank goodness you are here." Reaching out one hand, she grasped her friend's arm, a sense of weakness beginning to push through her frame. "I need a few moments to gather myself."

"Why?" Alarm sounded in Sophie's voice as she came closer to Lydia. "Whatever has happened?"

Lydia shook her head. "Nothing significant. It is only that I led the Duke to be introduced to Lady Ann – my mother and father's urging meant I had no other choice – and as we went to find her, the Duke said something that was a little... harsh. Though I said more than I should have done."

Her friend frowned, her eyes searching Lydia's. "What did you do?"

A sad smile pulled at Lydia's lips as she blinked back her tears. "I told him in no uncertain terms that I was not at all inclined to his company. That was spoken to him after he made it very clear indeed that he did not want to be in my company for any longer than was necessary. I spoke a little more bluntly than I ought, I will admit, but there was that arrogance that I found myself responding to."

"Oh, my dear Lydia." Sophie squeezed her hand. "I am sorry."

Lydia shook her head. "He made it plain that he did not believe that I was disinclined towards walking with him, perhaps thinking that any young lady would be glad of the attention it brought her whether or not she was pleased with the company itself, and I made sure to make my thoughts very plain in that regard."

Sophie winced but said nothing.

"Thereafter, he said that my parents ought to be ashamed of me." She could not help the tears as they fell, dropping her head so that she might hide her face from as many as she could. "My manner was much too blunt, my expressions too forward for someone such as the Duke of Melrose."

"That is an utterly dreadful thing for him to say!"

Sophie looked all around, as though she wanted to say something to the Duke directly only for Lydia to squeeze her hand again and pull her attention back.

"It may have been but I did my best to show no pain," she answered, managing to dry her tears. "Though I did tell him that I was a bluestocking and, therefore, my parents were already ashamed of me."

Sophie closed her eyes, shaking her head as she did so. "You should not have had such a thing said to you, my dear friend. The Duke ought to be better mannered than that."

Lydia took in a long breath and let herself settle inwardly, swallowing hard as the final few tears drained away. "I am quite myself again, I am sure."

Her friend gazed back at her for some moments, perhaps ascertaining whether or not such a thing was true. "Will you say something to the Duke?"

Fervently, Lydia shook her head no. "All I shall do is stay away from him," she answered, hating the wobble still in her voice. "And continue my research into his family so that I might complete my piece for The London Chronicle. Then, I shall forget all about him." Part of her now regretted pursuing the Duke of Melrose as her first subject for The London Chronicle but her study had already begun and she would not start again. Earlier that very afternoon, she and Sophie had visited not one but two libraries, as well as a bookshop that was more akin to a library than anything else! Subsequently, she now had not only a good deal of information about the area of England in which the Duke and his estate resided, but she had some books by which she intended to take on further study. Then, the article could be written, it could be sent to The London Chronicle, and her mind free then to release the Duke of Melrose entirely.

"That sounds wise to me." Sophie released her hand

though she continued to look into Lydia's face. "Are you sure you are quite all right?"

With a nod, Lydia gave a light toss of her head, her red curls catching the sunshine as they bounced. "I shall be, yes. Thank you, Sophie. You came just when I needed you."

PRESSING HER LIPS TIGHTLY TOGETHER, Lydia took the letter from the footman and tried to keep her gaze away from her mother's sharp eyes. "I thank you." The previous day, after the Duke's hard words to her, Lydia had found herself filled with a new determination – a determination to complete her piece of work on the Duke of Melrose just as quickly as she could. Thus, she had feigned a headache and had remained at home rather than go to the ball she had been expected to attend. In the hours she had garnered of solitude and silence – for both of her parents had gone to the ball after her promises that she would be quite all right – Lydia had read and read and read. She had found one or two rather interesting things, including a story that had made her eyebrows lift high in surprise. It had all been included in her article which, in the early hours of the morning, she had sent to The London Chronicle.

This, mayhap, was their reply.

"Is it a letter from a gentleman?" Lady Hampshire arched one eyebrow. "Lord Kendall, mayhap?"

Lydia shook her head. "I think it is from Sophie, Mama."

"Lord Kendall was present at the ball last evening." Much to Lydia's relief, her mother rose from her chair and made her way to the door. "Had you been present, then you would have been able to dance with him."

"I am sure another opportunity will soon become available," Lydia murmured, seeing her mother shake her head in evident desperation at Lydia's lack of interest in the gentleman before quitting the room entirely.

Relieved, Lydia broke the seal and unfolded the letter, tension grasping at her as she read the few short lines.

'Thank you for your article. We find it an excellent piece and would be glad to publish it in tomorrow's edition. As requested, we shall publish it under a gentleman's name rather than your own. Might we request another piece just as soon as you have one available?'

Her heart leaped, joy spread like fire across her chest and sent her smile wide. Jumping around the room, Lydia clasped the letter to her chest, twirling and spinning as though she were dancing with an invisible partner. The world opened up to her again, no longer closed, holding her only to propriety, to dancing, and to dull conversations with gentlemen where she pretended she was not what she truly was.

She could read! She could learn! She could write! And best of all, her work was valued and appreciated by others.

Lydia could think of nothing better.

∼

I DO wonder if he has anything on the history of St Albans. Lydia traced her fingers along the row of books, tilting her head this way and that as she kept one ear open for any of the other guests who might step into the room. She was attending Lord Montrose's soiree and though her friend, Lady Markham, was in attendance as well as other acquaintances, she had no interest in conversation and remarks about the weather. Her mind was racing, full of thoughts about the Duke and his family and just how well the article would be received by the *ton*. She knew that The London Chronicle had been published this afternoon. It would, by now, be in the hands of the *beau monde* but as yet, she did not know as to what society thought of it. Would it go unnoticed? Would there be only a few remarks made about it? Or was there *any* possibility that it would capture the attention of a good many of the gentlemen and ladies, making them eager for more?

Lydia tried to calm herself a little, pushing her thoughts to what area – and what family – she might write about next. The Duke of Melrose had been an interesting subject, for she had certainly discovered one or two things that had pricked her curiosity but whether or not she would find the same about another gentleman or lady, Lydia could not say. St Albans was an area known to her, and there were certainly many distinguished families from that area, but as yet, Lydia had not settled on anyone.

I wonder if –

Her heart slammed hard into her chest as the door to the library was pushed back, hard. She turned quickly, pushing her back against the shelves of books, pressing into the shadows for fear that she was about to witness something quite improper, or be set upon by a rogue, come in search of a lady alone.

Her fears faded as a gentleman staggered in, though Lydia recognized him at once. It was none other than the Duke of Melrose! He had one hand pressed against his forehead and was muttering under his breath, his shoulders a little hunched. With seeming irritation, he made to push the door shut but Lydia moved quickly, not wanting to be seen alone with him.

"Your Grace. If you would excuse me before you shut the door, then I would be grateful."

He started violently, his hand dropping to his side, peering at her. "Lady... Lady Lydia?"

"Melrose, are you quite all right?"

Before Lydia could answer, Lord Kendall stepped into the library, only to stop short at the sight of Lydia and the Duke together. His eyes widened but Lydia smiled quickly, gesturing to the door.

"Forgive me, Lord Kendall, I was just about to take my leave. The Duke stepped into the library without being aware of my presence."

Lord Kendall smiled quickly. "You sought some solitude in here, mayhap?"

She nodded, returned his smile, and made to leave, only for the Duke of Melrose to reach out and catch her hand.

"Wait."

A streak of fire tore up her arm and sent panic into her heart as she pulled her fingers out of his. Swallowing, she glanced at Lord Kendall but he was frowning hard, seemingly as confused as she was.

"I – I need to apologize." The Duke closed his eyes, his breathing ragged. "I spoke harshly to you and I must now apologize for it."

Lydia blinked in surprise. "Your Grace?"

"In the park, at the fashionable hour. I spoke sharply and without consideration and I can see that it must have been hurtful, despite your seeming lack of regard for my words." He held her gaze steadily as he drew himself up to standing tall again, his breathing seeming to slow and settle. "I sincerely apologize, Lady Lydia. I ought not to have said anything of the sort to you."

This was so utterly unexpected that for a long time,

Lydia did not know what to say. She simply gazed back at the Duke, wondering if he was intending to laugh at her when she accepted his apology, wondering if he meant to throw those words back in her face. But when he shook his head and looked away, rubbing one hand over his chin, slowly, she began to believe him.

"I am grateful to you for your acknowledgment of that," she said, her voice soft from surprise. "I will not pretend that I was not affected by what you said, Your Grace."

He looked back at her. "It will not happen again."

Lydia blinked, nodded, and then made to step away, only for something to tug at her heart. She looked back at the Duke, seeing how troubled he appeared and how his friend continued to frown in what, to her, looked like confusion and concern over the Duke's manner.

"Might I be so bold as to ask whether you are quite well, Your Grace?"

The Duke let out a quiet snort, his fingers pushing through his hair now. "No, I am not, Lady Lydia, but that is not your concern."

She frowned. "I am well aware of that, but I am only expressing concern for you."

"There is nothing you can do," he answered, looking to Lord Kendall now. "Nothing *any* of you can do. It is only I who can discover if what has been written is true."

A sudden fear clasped at Lydia's heart. "What has been written?"

He waved one hand at her, beginning to pace up and down the library. "You know of what I speak, I am sure. For everyone in the *ton* appears to have read The London Chronicle today."

CHAPTER SEVEN

Earlier that same evening.

HENRY SMILED into Lady Judith's eyes. She was, he considered, very beautiful indeed, though he did consider her conversation a little lacking. At times, he caught her glancing at her mother or her father, perhaps in the hope that they would help guide the conversation when she could not. Though, mayhap, she was merely a little overwhelmed by his presence and he could well understand that. He was a Duke, after all.

"And I hear you are well acquainted with our host for this evening, Your Grace?" she asked, as Henry nodded. "Are you related to the Marquess of Montrose?"

Henry smiled. "I think we are vaguely related but in truth, I cannot recall the connection. He hails from Scotland but comes to London for the Season every year, or so I have heard! His son, Lord Gellatly, is nearer to my age whereas Lord Montrose himself was well connected to my father."

"I see." Lady Judith did not seem to know what to say now, her eyes drifting away from him, and Henry, seeing it, let a small frown dart across his forehead.

"Might I interrupt? I know it is dreadfully rude of me but all the same, I feel as though I must do so!" When another gentleman came to join the conversation, Henry felt himself a trifle irritated, particularly when Lady Judith's eyes lit up with clear delight at seeing him. Henry tried his best not to let his scowl etch itself across his face in the way that it wished, reminding himself that this gentleman had just as much right to speak to Lady Judith as he.

"Lord Telford, are you acquainted with the Duke of Melrose?"

Henry waited for the fellow to shake his head, only for his eyebrows to lift as the gentleman nodded.

"Yes, I am." He bowed his head. "Good evening, Your Grace."

"Good evening, Lord Telford." Having no knowledge or insight coming to him about this fellow, Henry inclined his head and chose to step back. "I shall excuse myself and leave you to your conversation. Good evening."

Keeping a smile on his face, Henry made his way from Lady Judith's side, thinking to himself that he might go to call upon her to take tea the following day, only for another young lady to come towards him. Henry frowned, only to realize that he was already acquainted with this lady.

"Lady Markham." Glad that he had recalled her name, Henry bowed. "Good evening."

"Good evening, Your Grace." There was a slight tightness in her expression and, much to Henry's surprise, she came to step a little closer to him, her eyes searching his. "Might I say, Your Grace, that I am surprised to hear that you would speak so callously and unfeelingly to a young lady such as Lady Lydia?"

The unexpected nature of her conversation made Henry's stomach twist sharply. "I beg your pardon?"

"She has told me of what you said to her yesterday, at Hyde Park," Lady Markham continued, her eyes flashing. "Is it true that you stated her parents ought to be ashamed of her, merely because she did not show any sort of enjoyment at being in your company?"

A flush crept up Henry's neck and into his face. "I do not think that my conversation with Lady Lydia is any of your concern, Lady Markham."

"And I think it is." With tenacity, Lady Markham tipped up her chin, narrowing her eyes just a little. "Lady Lydia is my dearest and closest friend and when I find out that a Duke has made her cry with his harsh words, I am forced to do something!"

She was crying? Shame burst like a torrent over Henry's heart and he looked away, his face warm.

"You may not like the way that Lydia spoke to you, Your Grace, for no doubt, you expect *every* young lady to be filled with deference and delight at your company! However, that does not mean that you ought to speak with any sort of harshness towards her, does it? Or do you think that your standing means you can say what you please without hesitation?"

Henry shook his head. "No, I certainly do not think that."

"Then might I suggest that you consider what I have said and, thereafter, make an apology if you feel as though it is merited?" Her eyes still glinting with clear upset and anger which, Henry knew, was directed solely at him, Lady

Markham took a step back. "Lady Lydia is a very learned and passionate young lady and it is, to my mind, a great shame that her interests are not encouraged, simply because it is deemed incorrect for a young lady to have such passions." She tilted her head a fraction, her eyes gleaming. "I wonder if your opinion of her might change, Your Grace, if you were to consider a perspective other than your own."

A little irritated by Lady Markham's forwardness and her pricking questions, Henry's eyebrows fell heavily over his eyes. "And what do you mean by that?"

Lady Markham smiled but it held no warmth. "Only to say that to have such determined, fixed opinions means that you might miss out on a great deal, Your Grace. If you were truly to understand who Lydia is, then you might discover that while she is different from every other young lady in the *ton*, she is *different from every other young lady in the ton* – and that is a most remarkable thing."

Leaving Henry with his head filled with her final words, Lady Markham turned on her heel and walked away from him, making Henry frown after her. Yes, he knew that Lady Lydia was unlike any other young lady in London but that was why he disliked her so, was it not?

Unless she is suggesting that my dislike is misplaced.

Still frowning, Henry rubbed one hand over his forehead, gesturing to a nearby footman to bring him a drink. He was not used to his opinions being challenged in such a way but perhaps he was wrong to be so stagnant.

And I was certainly wrong in how I spoke to Lady Lydia yesterday. Sighing inwardly, Henry shook his head. *I shall have to find her and apologize.*

"Ah, there you are. I did wonder if you were in hiding."

Henry frowned as Lord Kendall came towards him. "Hiding?"

His friend nodded. "Yes. After what was written in The London Chronicle?"

A weight dropped into Henry's stomach. "There was something in the Chronicle written about me?"

His friend's eyebrows lifted. "You did not see it?"

"I did not."

"Oh." Lord Kendall shrugged and looked away. "It is nothing significant, of course."

Henry grimaced. "You are going to have to tell me what was said."

Lord Kendall glanced at him. "It was nothing of any importance. The writer has chosen to consider a certain area of England to write about and does so by not only mentioning the area itself and historical places of interest and the like but also a particular family. You were the chosen one for this article it seems."

There were no family secrets that Henry was afraid would be revealed though all the same, a trickle of sweat ran down his back. "What was written about me?"

With a small shrug, Lord Kendall struggled to meet his gaze, telling Henry that there was more to this story than his friend wanted to mention.

"Kendall."

With a long sigh, Lord Kendall glanced back at him and then looked away again. "There was some information about your late father, your mother and extended family as well as a little about your predecessors going back through history. That was interesting, of course, but I did not know the story about the stolen heirlooms. That was... difficult to read though the author did state that it was entirely whispers and nothing more."

"Stolen heirlooms?"

Lord Kendall nodded, his eyes rounding. "You do not know the story?"

Panic gripped Henry as he looked into his friend's face, filled with surprise, and felt fear shoot through him. "I must read this for myself." Grabbing a footman, he demanded a copy of The London Chronicle, turning back to wait with Lord Kendall. Everything in him seemed to be strung tight, his whole body burning as he waited for the footman to bring him the paper.

"It is only a story, recall," Lord Kendall said, quietly as Henry fought to keep from pacing in the drawing room, aware of just how much scrutiny it would bring. "A rumor. A whisper. That is all."

Henry said nothing, practically snatching the newspaper out of the footman's hand when he returned with it. It did not take long for him to find the article, his breathing becoming quicker by the second as he read through the lines.

'There is a story that the Duke of Melrose's heirlooms were lost and lost to a friend of the previous Duke. It is said that the late Duke of Melrose was returning home one evening, only to be stopped by a highwayman who stole the family heirlooms from him – heirlooms that he was bringing home from London. In the ensuing fight, the Duke struck the highwayman's face with his blade and escaped with his life! For any who believe it, the late Duke stated that the culprit was none other than the late Lord Harleton though this was never proven.'

"What?" Henry read over the lines again, trying to understand them, trying to make sense of all that he read. How could it be that his father had believed such a thing for years but had never told him of it? And how had the writer of this article found out when he had not had any awareness of it?

"I – I must – " Stalking blindly through the gathered crowd, Henry made his way through them with as much dignity as he could, suddenly determined for solace and solitude. This was an utter shock, for though he had always been told that the heirlooms had been lost but never that they had been stolen! He had not heard about the highwayman, had not been told that there had been a suspected theft and certainly had not understood that his father had believed it to be his close friend that would be akin to Henry accepting that Lord Kendall had done something truly dreadful! No, he could not accept it.

But if they are lost, then is it not my duty to find them again?

Pushing open the first door he saw, Henry strode into another room, lit only by the fire. Pushing one hand to his forehead, he paused for a moment, only to turn t make to shut the door, desirous only for his own company at present.

"Your Grace. If you would excuse me before you shut the door, then I would be grateful."

Henry started violently, his hand dropping to his side as he looked into the gloom, trying to ascertain who it was.

His stomach dropped. *Why does she have to be here, at this moment?* "Lady... Lady Lydia?"

"Melrose, are you quite all right?"

Henry glanced to his left, seeing Lord Kendall hurry in. His eyes went to Lady Lydia, rounding a little as though Henry had deliberately stepped inside to be in her company. That, or mayhap he was surprised at her lack of chaperone.

Lady Lydia pointed to the door. "Forgive me, Lord Kendall, I was just about to take my leave. The Duke stepped into the library without being aware of my presence."

With a small smile, Lord Kendall nodded. "You sought some solitude in here, mayhap?"

With a nod of her own, Lady Lydia made to quit the room but something in Henry forced him to step forward, to catch her hand in his. "Wait."

It was a command he gave her, of that he was well aware, but her presence here was the only opportunity he had to apologize for what he had done. Yes, his mind was filled with all that The London Chronicle had said but at the same time, he had not forgotten his responsibility here.

"I – I need to apologize." Henry closed his eyes as he spoke, feeling each word burning on his lips. He wanted to speak his apology quickly, desired only to have it spoken so that he might instead concentrate on the story in The London Chronicle. "I spoke harshly to you and I must now apologize for it."

"Your Grace?"

Confusion filled her voice and Henry opened his eyes, gritting his teeth for a moment over the fact that he would have to explain precisely what it was he meant. "In the park, at the fashionable hour. I spoke sharply and without consideration and I can see that it must have been hurtful, despite your seeming lack of regard for my words." He held her gaze, trying his best to prove, in both his standing and his tone, that he was genuine in his desire to express regret over his actions. "I sincerely apologize, Lady Lydia. I ought not to have said anything of the sort to you."

Silence was his only answer – and for some minutes, at that! Lady Lydia's eyes widened and Henry found himself a little struck by just how vivid they were. They were like emeralds, gleaming and pure. His breathing became a little steadier as he looked into her eyes; her presence seeming to calm him for some inexplicable reason. Henry felt his heart slow to a steadier pace, seeing Lady Lydia's expression soften just a little.

"I am grateful to you for your acknowledgment of that." She glanced away for a moment. "I will not pretend that I was not affected by what you said, Your Grace."

A fresh guilt ripped at his heart. Clearly, he had caused her more pain than he had recognized. "It will not happen again."

With another long look, she finally turned to make for the door, only to pause. "Might I be so bold as to ask whether you are quite well, Your Grace?"

Reminded of what it was that troubled him now that his apology was completed, Henry let out a low exclamation, pushing his fingers into his hair as he bowed his head. "No, I am not, Lady Lydia, but that is not your concern." He had not meant that to be harsh in any way but nor did he want her to trouble herself with matters that were not for her to know of.

"I am well aware of that, but I am only expressing concern for you."

Glancing at her, Henry rubbed one hand over his eyes again, aware that she had snapped back at him. Trying to gentle his voice, he shook his head. "No, there is nothing you can do." He looked to Lord Kendall, who was now frowning heavily. "Nothing *any* of you can do. It is only I who can discover if what has been written is true."

Lady Lydia pressed her lips together for a moment, then asked him the question he had seen in her eyes. "What has been written?

With a flick of his fingers, Henry began to pace, quite certain that almost everyone – Lady Lydia included –

would have read what was in The London Chronicle by now. "You know of what I speak, I am sure. For everyone in the *ton* appears to have read The London Chronicle today."

"Oh." The awareness in her voice made him grimace though he continued to pace, watching her now and again and wondering why she did not take her leave.

"It is only a story," Lord Kendall said, breaking the silence. "You did not know about this? About any of it?"

"No." Henry stopped pacing, looking desperately around the room. "Is there not some whisky or brandy here?"

"Let me get you something." For whatever reason, Lady Lydia was the one to move to get him what he desired, rather than Lord Kendall. She appeared to be quite determined to stay with them, clearly desirous to linger in this conversation rather than return to the others, though Henry chose not to question it.

"I remember you mentioned the heirlooms," Lord Kendall said, as Lady Lydia poured three glasses, making Henry's eyebrows lift. "But you never went into detail about them."

Henry scowled, looking down into the fire rather than at his friend. "I was always told that the heirlooms had gone missing and that I was not to speak of them. But this story now states that my father had them stolen by a highwayman?" He squeezed his eyes closed tightly, his breathing quickening again. "I do not understand why he would not tell me something like that, why he feared telling me the truth."

"Your Grace. Here."

Turning his head, Henry looked into Lady Lydia's face, taking the glass from her. Her eyes were filled with questions, worry playing about her mouth as she caught one lip between her teeth.

He did not understand why.

"I thank you." Taking the glass from her, he looked at the glass in her hand. "You also?"

The tone of surprise made a shadow dance across her expression. "Yes, Your Grace," came the reply. "I, on occasion, prefer a little glass of brandy rather than the usual tea or ratafia."

Henry considered this, about to state that he did not think it proper for a young lady to drink brandy, only to shake his head to himself and turn his gaze away. Was this not precisely what Lady Markham had suggested he do? That he keep his thoughts entirely to himself on such matters?

Besides, he thought to himself, *that is not something I need to be considering at this time.*

"It is only a story," she said, after a few moments, repeating the very same words as Lord Kendall. "That is all. A story. It does not mean that it has any truth to it. I am sure that the author thought only of the entertainment in the story rather than hoping it would cause you any distress."

Throwing back his brandy in one gulp, Henry caught his breath as fire poured into his lungs. "You do not understand, Lady Lydia," he rasped, barely able to look at her as he fought to breathe evenly. "The family heirlooms – diamonds – have been missing for many a year but my father would never tell me what happened. All he said was that they were lost."

"And maybe that is still true," she answered, evenly. "A story is nothing but that: a story."

Unsure as to why he was speaking with her so openly but finding himself unable to do anything but that, Henry shook his head. "I have always found myself frustrated and upset that there was nothing more to be said about the diamonds. Whenever they were mentioned, my father would close his mouth tightly and refuse to say a single word. Even when he became ill before he died, he refused to say anything to me about them. I do not know how they became lost, when and where such a thing took place – I know nothing whatsoever! And now to hear this story, a story I have never heard before in my life, makes my head spin with thoughts and wonderings and confusions!"

"You could write to your mother and ask her what she knows, if anything?" Lord Kendall came a little closer, concern clear in every inch of his expression. "I do not think I have ever seen you like this, Melrose. I knew that the lost heirlooms troubled you but never to this extent."

"I have sat on my frustration for many a year," Henry muttered, setting his glass down on a table before sinking into a chair, putting his head in his hands as energy drained slowly out of him. "I cannot quite believe that this has happened. How did the author – whoever it was – find out such a thing when I knew nothing of it?"

Lord Kendall came to sit beside him as Lady Lydia slowly stepped back, seeming to desire the shadows rather than any sort of nearness.

"I do not know but you can ask him yourself," Lord Kendall answered. "The name of the author is written in The London Chronicle. All you need do is find him."

"Then I shall," Henry stated, his hand curling into a fist before slamming into his open palm. "And I shall not rest until I have answers."

CHAPTER EIGHT

"I do not know what to do!"

Sophie held up one hand as Lydia paced up and down in the drawing room. "You first must calm yourself."

"Calm myself? I cannot!" Throwing up her hands, Lydia shook her head, her breathing growing faster as she tried to fight the panic in her chest. "The Duke of Melrose is going to write to The London Chronicle to demand an address for the author of that piece and they will give it to him!"

"They will not." Sophie smiled gently as Lydia turned to face her friend, the calm expression on her face doing nothing to quieten Lydia's frayed nerves. "What name did you give to the Chronicle?"

Lydia swallowed. "Mr. Adam Smith."

This made Sophie's smile grow. "A very plain name, I must say." She patted the seat beside her to encourage Lydia to join her but Lydia did not, feeling everything in her burning with fear and fright. "You made it quite clear in your letter that you had to be protected and The London

Chronicle will do that. They have done it in the past and they shall do it again."

"How can you be sure?"

Sophie smiled gently. "Because I am friends with another young lady who, at one time, did the very same thing as you, albeit in a different form. The London Chronicle did not reveal her name to anyone. Besides which, The London Chronicle has ladies guiding its publication and the like and they know very well what might occur should they give out your name to anyone who asks, even though you have asked to be known as Adam Smith! They will not do it, not even for a Duke. I can assure you of that."

A slow winding relief began to pull at Lydia's overwhelming concerns, beginning to settle within her as she nodded slowly, her eyes closing for a moment as she fought to find a steadiness within herself.

"You need not worry in that regard," her friend assured her again. "Come now, sit down and tell me what your thoughts are."

Feeling a little fatigued now, Lydia did as she was bade and went to sit beside her friend, only for a cup of tea to be pushed into her hands. Taking a sip, she closed her eyes and tried to regain a hold of her thoughts.

"When I saw the Duke's reaction to my article, I was utterly overcome with confusion and fright," she began, remembering how the Duke had stormed up and down the library, flinging his arms up as he spoke. "Not for one moment did I ever think that he was unaware of this story!"

"Where did you find it?"

"In the library," Lydia admitted. "There is a section where papers, old bets and, to be truthful, nothing but gossip from years past is still kept securely. I am not one for gossip and rumour but I did think that such a story might be interesting enough for the article. It did not have scandal and shame attached to it, for such a thing would never do!"

"Indeed not." Sophie took a sip of her tea and then set the cup down. "I must say, I personally thought that the article was written very well indeed. I did not know anything of what you wrote."

Lydia smiled ruefully. "I thank you."

"And are you going to continue writing?"

Closing her eyes, Lydia considered for a few moments. "I had thought to, *before* the Duke reacted as he did. I was wondering if I could find any history from St Albans, for there are many distinguished families from that area which is why I was in the library last evening in the first place! It was very well stocked and I could not help myself, especially when I had been able to escape from my mother's watchful eye for a time!"

"Indeed." Sophie chuckled gently. "I would have expected nothing less from you. Though," she continued, her smile fading, "if I might be able to offer you some advice, might I suggest that it is imperative that you continue to write?"

Blinking in surprise, Lydia frowned. "Imperative?"

"Else the Duke might think that you have chosen him for a purpose," her friend replied. "He might believe that the article was written solely for that story about the missing heirlooms, that it was written by the very person who took them – or lost them – or some such thing, to injure him."

A gasp caught in Lydia's throat as she saw what her friend meant. "You are quite right. I cannot do such a thing as that!"

"No, you cannot."

"Then I must write," Lydia agreed, nodding to herself as she reached for her tea again. "My study must continue."

"Yes, it must." Sophie reached out and pressed Lydia's hand. "And you must not fear the Duke of Melrose. He will not discover your name."

Lydia nodded slowly, though her heart ached as she recalled just how troubled the Duke had appeared when he had been in the library. There had been frustration, upset, anger, and sorrow in him - she had seen all of them in his expression, his manner, and his voice. Did she not owe him the truth of how she had found that article in the first place? It had been an honest mistake on her part, yes, but that did not mean that she could not seek to make amends in some way.

Could I do it without revealing that I am the one who wrote the article?

Frowning, she set her tea cup down and rubbed between her eyebrows, thinking hard. The Duke already knew that she was a bluestocking, given that she had told him directly, so could she not simply state that she had found the story during her reading and study? That it had simply been an accidental find? Biting her lip, Lydia let out a breath of frustration, uncertain as to whether or not the Duke would believe her.

But I feel as though I must do something, she thought to herself, fully aware of her friend's scrutinizing expression though Lydia herself remained silent, choosing not to share her thoughts with Sophie. *Even if it is to relieve my own upset.*

"Are you going to tell me what you are thinking?"

Lydia smiled briefly at her Sophie, then shook her head. "Not as yet. But I think I shall take your advice and continue with my next article." So saying, she gestured to the door. "Might you wish to take a turn through London with me? My mother knows that I am here with you and she will not know if we were to step out."

"Step out to one of the bookshops or libraries, mayhap?" Sophie chuckled as Lydia nodded. "I should be glad to. Was it St Albans you were looking at?"

In answer to her friend's question, Lydia rose to her feet. "Indeed."

"Then I shall be glad to aid you in your search for information so you might write your next article." Coming to stand beside Lydia, Sophie embraced her tightly for a moment. "Set your concern aside. The matter with the Duke is over and done with already!"

Keeping her smile fixed, Lydia nodded though her thoughts went in an entirely different direction.

And yet, I feel as though matters with the Duke have only just begun.

"THERE NOW. IS THAT NOT BETTER?"

Lydia chuckled as she looked around what was one of the largest bookshops in all of London. Hatchards, with its many floors and a plethora of all manner of books and more, made her heart squeeze with delight. She had been here many times before and it never failed to take her breath away when she stepped inside. Sophie felt the same, she knew, and that had clearly been her sole reason for bringing her here. "We can hide away here for many an hour, I am sure."

"Indeed we can! Though your mother will require you home soon enough, will she not?"

Lydia considered, shrugging lightly. "I have an hour, mayhap. That should be more than enough time to find a history of St Albans."

Sophie smiled. "Then shall we begin?"

Approaching one of the curved staircases, Lydia began her climb, a thrill of joy racing up her spine as she moved to the next floor. This bookshop held all manner of delights for her, delights which she could not fully express though she knew that Sophie understood it all. Her joy faded a little as she considered her parents, wishing that they too might have understood even a modicum of her happiness in being surrounded by so many books and so much knowledge but she knew that would never happen.

Her lips twisted as she moved to the left of the stairs, ready to begin her search. Her love of learning had brought her nothing but contentment thus far but now, seeing what it had done to the Duke of Melrose, that gave her pause. She would have to be a good deal more careful now in what she wrote.

Looking at one shelf and then another, Lydia picked up her first book and soon, she was lost in what she was reading. The history of St Albans was fascinating enough, but there were mentions made of families in the area, of the chalk river that ran through it as well as the population increase – or in some years, a decrease. She began to wonder why that might have been, considering the land and the fields and debating inwardly whether there had been good rain some years and too much the next!

"Lady Lydia?"

Turning, Lydia caught her breath as the Duke of Melrose inclined his head to her, though his gaze never left hers. "Your Grace. I – I hope that you are well?" Her breathing suddenly became shallow as the Duke's gaze went to the book in her hand, making her snap it closed and hold it tightly to herself, fearful that he would see the title of it and, once the article was written, make the connection to her.

"I am better than I was yesterday, that much is true." The Duke managed a small smile, though he looked away from her as he spoke. "I have come in search of books that will help me find out the truth about my heirlooms, though whether or not I am looking in the right place, I do not know."

Lydia's eyebrows lifted. "You do not know where to look, then?"

The Duke's lips flattened, a flash of some unexplained emotion in his eyes. "I am not a gentleman used to bookshops and the like. Nor am I particularly inclined towards studying or seeking out specific information."

"I can help you if you wish." Lydia closed her eyes briefly the very moment she spoke, wondering why she had said such a foolish thing. It was not something she wanted to do, was it? Or was it only that her own inner upset and perhaps a twinge of guilt made her want to do something to bring him – and herself – a little peace?

The Duke frowned. "Lady Lydia, I am well aware of your... bluestocking ways and I do not think it in the least bit proper. It would not serve me well to have a lady such as yourself assist me in this."

Any hint of guilt washed away in a single moment as fire burst in her heart, her face flaming hot. "I beg your pardon?" She took a step closer to him, her eyes narrowing just a fraction as she fought to keep her voice low and steady. "Your Grace, *you* may consider it improper for a lady to be a bluestocking but that is nothing but your own prejudice. Tell me, what is so dreadfully wrong for a lady to be learned? What possible trouble could there be for a young lady to be knowledgeable and wise – two characteristics that you desire for yourself, no doubt? What protestation will you make against a lady who wants to learn about the world she lives in and all the wonderful things there are within it?"

At this, the Duke of Melrose lifted his chin, set his shoulders back, and opened his mouth... only to snap it closed again as a heavy frown settled across his forehead, dropping his eyebrows low over his eyes. The next moment, he ran one hand over his chin, looking away from her as his shoulders dropped and a sense of triumph began to climb over Lydia. She let the edge of her mouth lift up, the anger within her quickly fading away as she saw the Duke struggle to find his answer. He could not give her one, it seemed, and that sent a thrill right through her.

"I do not think it is something that a young lady needs to do," was all he said, though that did not seem to satisfy him – and certainly did not satisfy Lydia either! "Though I cannot give you a particular reason as to why that might be. Not as yet, anyway." This was added with a severity in his voice, as though he *would* find a reason and would tell her of it just as soon as he could, though that in itself made Lydia laugh. This made the Duke's eyebrows lift. "You think to mock me?"

Lydia shook her head. "No, not in the least, Your Grace, though I do find it quite remarkable that a gentleman with such a set opinion cannot find a *reason* for his belief. That is a little strange, is it not?"

The Duke's lips pulled to one side and he looked away. A long moment of silence passed before, finally, he conceded. "Yes, I suppose it is. And it is not the first time that I have been challenged to consider my own actions and standings." His chin lifted again as his hazel eyes swirled with thoughts, looking back into her face. "I am not too proud a gentleman to say that I shall never give a single consideration to all that I think and say, Lady Lydia. So, in that regard, I accept your offer to assist me in my search."

That took the smile from Lydia's face in an instant, her triumph evaporating. She had not thought that the Duke would turn around and say such a thing, had believed that he would be quite determined to cling to his idea that a bluestocking ought not to even be in his company! Now, however, she was stuck in this place where she had offered her help and could not now take that away from him.

"Lady Lydia?"

She licked her lips. "Yes, Your Grace. Of course." There was nothing else for her to say, nothing whereby she could refuse or take back her offer of assistance. "I would be glad to help you find the truth if you desire it."

He nodded, looking away from her again. "All I want to know is if this story is true and to do that, I must know where it came from. I have written to my mother to find out what she knows and also to The London Chronicle, though their answer came back to me very quickly indeed."

"Oh?" Lydia's voice grew higher in pitch as she waited for the Duke to explain, her own heart pounding furiously as nodded, noting the slight frown on his forehead. Would he not have already stated that he knew very well that *she* was the one responsible if he had come into that knowledge already?

"They would not say anything more to me." The frown on the Duke's forehead deepened. "It was most frustrating. They stated that the article came from a Mr. Adam Smith which is clear – to me, at least – that it is not the true name of the author!" He snorted. "No doubt some gentleman is hiding himself away from the *ton* for fear that some – such as I, mayhap – will turn against him because of his writings.

There is certainly a flair to the writing, however." A wry smile touched his lips. "It was very well written, I shall admit, with excellent knowledge of the area and the like. I can admit that without stating that I was pleased by what was said about the heirlooms."

Lydia swallowed tightly, wondering if she ought to confess the truth, right then and there. It went against everything she felt within, her mind kicking against the idea as though to shatter it. She dragged in air as the Duke's gaze steadied on hers, not at all certain what his reaction would be if she told him the truth. Would he step back from her, horrified? Or would he be angry with her?

And yet, the desire to be honest grew all the same. What good would it be to hide it from him? It was clear that this gentleman was in a good deal of distress and, given that he had now said he would accept her offer of aid, could she really push herself deeper into deception? She would have to pretend that she had found the story of the heirlooms instead of knowing precisely where it was, and that would be nothing short of placing lie upon lie. Would telling him the truth be worse than that? She did not want to lie, did not want to be dishonest but yet, at this present juncture, it did seem like the safest thing to do.

I cannot hide this from him. Her mind steadied on one single thought and she let out her breath slowly, recognizing that, if she told him here, he would not be able to explode in temper given their present situation.

"You have accepted my offer of help," she said, aware that her voice was shaking, "and while I am still willing to offer it, there is something more than I must tell you."

"Oh?" With a lift of his eyebrow, the Duke took a step closer and suddenly, Lydia could not even think about breathing. She could not look away from him, could not even think what she was going to say to him. Was it fear that coursed through her now? Or something more?

"Lady Lydia?" For the first time, the Duke's tone gentled as he moved a little away from her again, perhaps seeing how his presence had affected her. "I do not mean to push you, forgive me."

She shook her head, closing her eyes as she swallowed at the knot in her throat. "It is quite all right," she rasped, a little hoarsely. "It is only to say that I know where I can find the story about the heirlooms." Opening her eyes, she saw the shock flare in his eyes, his whole body starting in surprise at her words. "I can take you to it."

For some moments, nothing was said between them. The Duke appeared to be frozen in place, his eyes wide and staring as she pressed her lips tightly together in an attempt to keep the slight tremble in her frame at bay.

"The story?" With a sudden quickness, the Duke of Melrose came closer to her, his hand going to hers and grasping it tightly, making her shudder with fright as the awareness of what she had to say burned in her chest. "How can you find it? I do not understand."

Now I must tell him the truth.

It would do her no good to hide it, Lydia realized, for if she was to help him then she would *have* to tell him this regardless and to go on in their connection, to strengthen it only to then break it apart with the truth of what she had done would only bring disaster.

"I know because... " Shuddering visibly, she kept her gaze away from him. "I know because I am Adam Smith."

CHAPTER NINE

Henry could not quite take in what Lady Lydia had said. The words she spoke seemed to run away from him, avoiding him entirely. A heavy weight seemed to sink into his soul as he looked into her eyes, seeing how she could only glance at him once, twice, and then turn her head entirely away.

"You must forgive me, Lady Lydia." With a shake of his head, Henry frowned, hard. "I must not have heard you correctly."

Her voice was quiet, her head lowering now. "I think that you did, Your Grace."

"I cannot have done!" Henry's stomach twisted. "I was sure that you said that *you* were the writer for The London Chronicle but I must have misheard you."

Slowly, Lady Lydia lifted her chin and looked back into his eyes, a steadiness there that he had not expected to see. "You did not mishear me, Your Grace," she said, speaking much more clearly now. "It is just as I have said. I am the one who wrote the article, the one who is, at this very moment, engaging in some study for the next one I am to write." A slight shake ran through her but she did not look away from him. "I am the one who not only found but included the story about your family's heirlooms, though I meant no harm by it. I presumed that you already were aware of it."

Henry's heart clattered in his chest as he stared at Lady Lydia, barely able to accept what it was she was saying. Could it be just as she had said?

"You already know that I am a bluestocking." There seemed to be a greater confidence in Lady Lydia's voice now, as though the relief that she felt in speaking to him now filled her. "There is nothing in this that surprises you, surely?"

Raking one hand through his hair, Henry turned bodily away from her, trying to keep his shock from taking a complete hold of him. How could it be that this young lady was the writer of such a strong article? Yes, he knew that bluestockings were young ladies eager to possess as much learning as they could, but never once had he thought that such a creature would be able to write with such flair! It had not even come as a thought to his mind that a lady would be the author!

"I can show you where I found the story about your heirlooms," he heard Lady Lydia say. "And I am truly sorry for the distress that my article caused you. I hope you believe me when I state that I had no intention for there to be any sort of pain or upset caused by what I wrote."

Henry threw her a look, then shook his head, still keeping himself away from her. "It has come as a great shock to me to hear this from you, Lady Lydia. Though I shall admit that I do believe there was no malice involved. You did not have the intention to cause me pain, I can recognize that."

The relief that came from her was almost palpable. "I thank you."

"I – I need to take a little time." It was rather shameful to admit such a thing to her but his mind was so clouded that Henry recognized it would not be wise to say or do anything at this present time. "I must think a little more. That is all."

"Of course." A little boldly, Henry thought, Lady Lydia moved closer to him, her eyes lifting to his, her cheeks scarlet. "I am more than willing to show you where I found that story, Your Grace, even if you do not wish for my help in any other way. I understand that you must be astonished at my revelation but I am glad that I told you. I have been greatly concerned about it ever since I saw your reaction to the story."

This is why she lingered with myself and Lord Kendall in the library.

Henry nodded. "I understand."

"I shall take my leave of you now." Lady Lydia touched his arm briefly and something kicked hard in Henry's stomach. "Good afternoon, Your Grace."

Watching her, Henry only inclined his head rather than saying anything more. His chest felt tight, his stomach writhing as he tried to gather himself.

I am meant to go to call on Lady Judith, he reminded himself. *I cannot let this revelation prevent me from doing so.* He tried to tear his thoughts away from Lady Lydia and instead, concentrate on Lady Judith, attempting to bring her to mind but it was more than a little difficult. The only reason he had stopped at this bookshop was in the hope of finding some books relating to his family and his home but instead, he had stumbled upon such a great revelation that it was almost too much for him to take in!

Closing his eyes, Henry bent his head and took in three long breaths in the hope of steadying himself. He *had* to take his mind from the lady, *had* to forget all that she had said until his meeting with Lady Judith was brought to an end. He would make a fool of himself otherwise.

"What did think you of that, Your Grace?"

Henry blinked quickly, aware that he had been asked a question but that he had no knowledge whatsoever as to what it related to. "I – I think that it merits a good deal of consideration," he answered, seeing how Lady Judith and her mother exchanged a look as he spoke. "I am not a gentleman who would give any answer unless I had considered it for a long time." He had no idea whether or not this answer pertained in any way as to what had been asked but he had attempted to cover his lack of attention in any way he could.

"I see." Lady Kent smiled though there was clear confusion in her eyes. "I thought that all gentlemen adored hunting. I confess I am surprised to hear that you would consider Lord Berkshire's hunt for such a long time before attending."

Heat tore up Henry's frame. "Yes, well, I – I would have to think upon my other duties and responsibilities and the like before I chose whether to attend. I am sure you are well aware, Lady Kent, of the requirements that fall heavily upon gentlemen of a certain standing!" He winced inwardly, hearing himself sounding not only a little arrogant but also a trifle condescending as though he was berating Lady Kent in some way. Trying to smile so that she would not think he was doing such a thing, he lifted his shoulders. "I always give great consideration to any decision I make, even if I *do* like the hunt a great deal."

"I understand what you mean, Your Grace." Lady Kent's smile remained though, to Henry's mind, there was a certain tightness there. "My daughter and I fully understand and acknowledge that a gentleman's time is important."

"Of course." Lady Judith looked away from Henry, reaching for her tea at the same time. "Are there any other hobbies that you enjoy, Your Grace, aside from hunting when you can spare the time?"

Henry frowned gently. "I suppose that I enjoy good company," he replied, trying to think about what else it was that he enjoyed but, for whatever reason, struggling to find any clarity of thought. "Good conversation is of great importance to me."

Lady Judith nodded and sipped at her tea but said nothing more. Henry licked his lips, wondering what he ought to say and berating himself silently for his lack of clarity when it came to finding words for this conversation. Ever since he had come to join Lady Judith and her mother, he had battled against his thoughts, feeling them pulling towards Lady Lydia with an ever increasing strength.

"I am sure that you must have been a little surprised at the article in The London Chronicle."

Henry's gaze shot back to Lady Judith as she set her teacup down. "I did not know that your family heirlooms had been stolen. That must be very distressing for you."

"That is a story and nothing more," Henry snapped, seeing Lady Judith's eyes flare wide in surprise. "The family heirlooms were lost, they were not stolen." He spoke more harshly than he had intended but the words came still, not held back as he might otherwise have done. His thoughts were frayed, his heart pounding as all that Lady Lydia had told him stormed back into his mind. "I know who wrote the article and they have assured me that it was nothing more than a story that they discovered themselves. It has no basis in truth and I am disappointed to hear that you believe it, Lady Judith."

This made Lady Judith blink rapidly and Henry, seeing it, instantly closed his eyes, frustrated with himself for his quick words and harsh honesty. He had not needed to say such a thing.

"Your Grace." Lady Kent's voice was firm and as Henry looked back at her, he saw the heavy frown which drew a line down between her eyebrows. "My daughter was only trying to express her sorrow at the loss of your family heirlooms. Yes, it might well be a story but it was written in such a way as to make us *all* believe that it was the truth. I do not think that she needs to be berated in such a way."

Henry opened his mouth to say that she was quite correct and to, thereafter, make an apology, only for Lady Judith to toss her head and look away from him, showing more spirit than he had ever seen.

"It appears to me that there is a distinct lack of manners and consideration in this conversation, Mama," she said, now appearing to ignore Henry completely. "Might I be excused? I think I should like a few minutes to compose myself."

Letting out a low groan at his foolishness, Henry made to rise to his feet but a knock at the door interrupted him.

"Lord Telford, my lady."

Having been announced by the butler – and expected by Lady Judith given the immediate smile on her face and the way she practically jumped to her feet – Lord Telford stepped into the room and Henry forced himself to rise. It was more than evident to him now that Lady Judith had a distinct interest in Lord Telford and, evidently, no interest in him. And this despite the fact that he had a higher title, better standing, and, no doubt, a greater fortune!

Though it is not as though I have behaved as well as he.

"Lord Telford, how *good* to see you." Lady Judith sent Henry a sidelong glance as she welcomed the gentleman. "I am already looking forward to our conversation, for I know it will be a very pleasing one indeed."

Henry dropped his head and shut his eyes briefly, only to lift his head and force a smile. "I shall take my leave so that I do not interrupt this conversation," he said, with a nod to Lady Kent who did not appear to be in the least bit sorry that he was to take his leave of them. "Good afternoon."

"Good afternoon, Your Grace."

With every step heavier than the last, Henry made his way from the room and then back towards his waiting carriage. He had made a fool of himself, that much was clear. He had spoken with harshness and inconsideration, reacting badly to her mention of the heirlooms. It was only because it had been so fresh in his mind that he had responded so, Henry told himself, though in his heart, he still felt a great weight of guilt.

I truly have behaved poorly. Sitting back in his carriage, Henry let out a long sigh and rested his head back against the squabs. As he did so, the many instances when he had spoken harshly to Lady Lydia came back to him, reminding him of just how many other times he had failed to behave as he ought. His lips pulled downwards, his guilt growing all the greater as he realized just how poorly he had met the standards required of a gentleman. Could he truly expect any young lady to match all of his requirements when it came to his consideration of a bride when he was himself so dreadful a failure in so many ways?

"I do not know what to do." Speaking aloud, Henry lifted his head and looked out of the carriage window, trying to pluck out his thoughts one at a time. He had the requirements for a wife still sitting there, though quite how he was to seek courtship when he had nothing but the heirlooms in his mind, he did not know! Trying to make a match whilst attempting to find out the truth about the heirlooms *and* seeking to better himself and his character seemed to be a heavy weight indeed!

"Though I have Lady Lydia's help in the former," he muttered, sitting back again and letting his mouth curve in a rueful smile. That had been a most unexpected revelation *and* an unexpected offer of help and he had even surprised himself in accepting it!

Mayhap being willing to consider the opinions of others to be of value aside from just his own, as Lady Markham had stated to him only a few days ago, might, in fact, bring him a little more clarity of mind and open his world up a little more.

The only thing Henry had to decide was whether he was truly willing to do such a thing or not.

CHAPTER TEN

"*Thank you for your third article. It will be published within the sennight. We look forward to your fourth piece for us.*" So saying, Lydia looked back at her friend, her shoulders lifting and then falling again. "It seems as though The London Chronicle is willing to continue publishing what I write."

Sophie smiled. "That is good, is it not?"

"It is." Lydia looked away, then sighed. "It seems a strange thing even to admit but I have had my thoughts centered solely on the Duke of Melrose this last sennight." She let out another sigh, frustrated with herself for having so much time given up to thinking about him. "It has been almost seven full days since we were last in company together, when he came to the bookshop and where I revealed the truth to him."

"Something I still cannot quite believe that you did," her friend interjected, a quiet smile on her lips. "You went against everything that you had already determined to do and found great courage to be truthful with him although he could have not only revealed you to the *ton* but also railed at you loudly and publicly for what you had written!"

"But he did not," Lydia answered. "And though he did speak to me once I had told him the truth, he has not come in search of me since. I thought he would."

Sophie nodded. "As did I. I thought in his desperation to find out the truth about the heirlooms, he would have come in search of you."

Lydia lifted her shoulders and then let them fall. "Mayhap he has decided to continue with the search alone." She did not know why, could certainly not even attempt to explain it either to Sophie or even to herself but there was something that upset her about that silence. It was as though part of her *wanted* him to come to speak with her, even though she found his presence overbearing and irritating.

"But you have been able to concentrate on your articles," Sophie said, with a small shrug. "That is a good thing, at least."

"It is. Helped by your presence and your willingness to take me to the various bookshops and libraries!" Lydia laughed, as Sophie chuckled. "My mother would never permit such a thing if she knew of it."

Sophie grinned. "It is just as well that she does not! Though I am concerned that as yet, no gentlemen have come to call on you." Her smile began to fade. "That will trouble your mother, will it not? After all, she knows that I have introduced you to my acquaintances, and yet... "

"That is because I refuse to show them any interest," Lydia answered, with a roll of her eyes. "Yes, many of them do not appear to care whether one is a bluestocking or not but these same gentlemen seem to be quite unable to have a prolonged conversation about anything other than shooting, hunting, or the local gossip!" She had tried, during her dances at various balls or in conversation at soirees, to bring the conversation around to weightier matters but none of them had been successful. Her remarks had either been met with silence or turned around to suit whatever it was that the specific gentleman she spoke with was interested in.

"All the same, I do think – "

"Ah, Lady Markham. You are come to call again."

Lydia and Sophie's conversation was brought to a swift close as none other than Lady Hampshire swept into the room, her eyes sharp – and Lydia's stomach twisted. Clearly, her mother was in some sort of temper today and Lydia feared she would soon bear the brunt of it.

"I had hoped that you would have someone *other* than Lady Markham calling, Lydia." Lady Hampshire came to join them both, giving Lydia a somewhat disapproving look as she did so. "But alas, it is still only Lady Markham!"

"I was just about to suggest that we go into town," Sophie answered, a smile on her face which Lydia knew she did not really feel. "There will be many of the *ton* present at this hour."

Lady Hampshire's lip curled. "I am not certain that it will bring any hope to the present situation, Lady Markham. My daughter does not appear to be attracting the interest of any gentlemen and that concerns me. Even Lord Kendall, who has danced with her and spoken at length on occasion, has never come to call."

Lydia fought the urge to either shrug or respond with sharp words of her own, wanting to state that she had no interest in whether or not Lord Kendall had come to take tea, for though he was a handsome and considerate gentleman, it was clear to her that he was looking for something more than she was willing to give.

"I think that – " Letting out a breath of frustration at the knock which came to the door, Lady Hampshire called for the servant to enter. Her eyes still lingered on Lydia as the footman came in, bearing a card which he handed directly to Lady Hampshire.

Her gaze fell to it and Lydia shared a look with Sophie, silently wondering how she might escape from her mother's harsh words and clear intentions to have her *do* something to garner the interest of a gentleman.

Then, Lady Hampshire gasped, her eyes flaring wide as she gazed back at Lydia. "The Duke of Melrose is come to call!"

Lydia blinked quickly, a tightness in her chest as she clasped her hands tightly together in her lap, something like relief flooding through her.

"Send him in at once!" Lady Hampshire exclaimed, rising to her feet and practically shooing the footman out of the room. "Hurry now!" Turning, she came towards Lydia who also got to her feet. "Oh, if only you'd chosen your best dress! This is certainly *not* the right color for you, for – "

"It is perfectly all right, Mama," Lydia answered, refusing to let her mother fuss over her and desperately hoping that she would not take the Duke's presence for interest. Lydia knew precisely why he was here. "Hurry now. He will come any moment."

The door opened again before Lady Hampshire had a chance to return to her seat and in a moment, the Duke walked into the room, a heavy set expression on his face as he took them in. His gaze lingered on Lydia for a moment before he bowed, making her shiver in fear of what the darkness on his face might mean.

"Thank you for permitting me to call unexpectedly," he said, no smile on his face.

"But of course, Your Grace!" Lady Hampshire's voice was filled with excitement and inwardly, Lydia winced. "Do you wish to join us? We were just about to take tea."

"I will not, I thank you."

"Oh." Lady Hampshire's face fell in an instant, though Lydia continued to hold the Duke's gaze, wondering what his purpose was in coming to call. "Then might I ask – "

"Lady Lydia," the Duke interrupted, though Lydia presumed he had not meant to. "I wondered if you would join me for a ride in the carriage? I understand this is a little unexpected and if you have intentions for this afternoon already, then – "

"She does not. Of course, she would be glad to join you!" Lady Hampshire waved one hand at Lydia, gesturing her to the door. "Though she will need a chaperone."

"Lady Markham?" Lydia spoke quickly before her mother could place herself in that position. "Would you care to join us? I know that my mother has Lady Gillingham expected later this afternoon."

Lady Markham nodded and smiled, moving towards the door as Lady Hampshire began to stammer. "But of course."

"Thank you, Your Grace." Lydia inclined her head for a moment and then came towards her mother, grasping her hand briefly and seeming to pull her from her confusion. "I will not be too long, Mama. Lady Markham shall be a perfect chaperone, I can assure you."

It took Lady Hampshire a moment but eventually, she smiled. "Of course. Do enjoy yourself, my dear." She looked to the Duke, a dazzling smile on her face now. "Thank you for your consideration of my daughter, Your Grace. I hope that you have a wonderful drive together."

Heat seared Lydia's cheeks as she made her way to the door, fully aware of her mother's expectations about this carriage ride. The Duke had not called to have her for her company alone, he clearly was expecting her to take him to the library – or wanted to tell her that he no longer thought it wise to have her help. It did not take her long to make her way to the carriage, the Duke handing up both herself and Sophie. The ladies sat together and Lydia found herself grateful for Sophie's company. The Duke's presence was unnerving enough!

"Thank you for joining me." The Duke's hazel eyes gazed back into Lydia's, never once turning to Sophie as the carriage remained still, waiting for the Duke's direction as to where they were to go. "I presume that your friend knows all?"

"Yes, I do," Sophie spoke smartly, ignoring the Duke's frown. "I am present, Your Grace, and you can speak to me directly."

Much to Lydia's surprise, the Duke did not state that he had done nothing wrong nor berate Lady Markham for her forwardness. Instead, he nodded, his jaw tightening for just a moment.

"You are quite correct, Lady Markham. I should have addressed you directly." He offered a thin smile. "Forgive me. My thoughts have been a little tormented of late and I am not as genteel as I ought to be."

Sophie's eyebrows lifted, as did Lydia's. She had never heard him speak in such a way before, though he had apologized to *her* some time ago, she recalled. But there was a gentleness of manner now, a quick awareness that he was not as he ought to be and his willingness to admit it outright was quite refreshing.

"Lady Lydia," he continued, turning his attention again to her. "I hope that you might still be willing to show me where you found this story?"

She nodded. "Of course. It is in Fellows' Circulating Library."

"Then there we shall go." It took the Duke a few moments to tell the driver where to direct the carriage but after that, he sat back in his seat and, much to Lydia's surprise, smiled at her. It was the first genuine smile he had ever offered her and, seeing it, Lydia felt her heart lift. There was a kindness in his smile, something that lit his expression with a brightness that hadn't been there before in any prior conversations. It was as if, in speaking with her and in finding where they were to go, he now felt a new sense of relief and mayhap, even a resolve.

"I have not often been to the library." The Duke glanced away from her. "I presume you have been there many a time?"

"When I can, yes." Lydia smiled at Sophie. "I have Lady Markham to attend with me, which has made things a good deal easier since neither my mother nor father would permit me to go."

"Though I have heard it can often be seen as a social setting?" With a question dancing in his eyes, the Duke looked back towards her. "They would not be willing for you to attend even then?"

Lydia shook her head, a sadness touching her heart. "Even still, Your Grace. They know very well that I do not delight in novels or gossip. Instead, I lend myself to weightier things, to learning and to study and that is not something that they encourage in the least. Though I am sure you can understand that, given that you agree with them."

The light that had been in the Duke's expression slowly began to fade as Lydia spoke, though she did not regret what had been said. He had already made it clear that he did not think much of bluestockings and Lydia was simply repeating that back to him.

The Duke cleared his throat gruffly then gestured to Lady Markham. "I believe that it was you, Lady Markham, who challenged me to consider my opinions a little less and think on others a little more, to consider another perspective instead of believing that all I think and determine is correct. These last few days, I have been challenged to do so, for I have not only discovered that Mr. Adam Smith was not a gentleman, as I had considered, but a young lady! And I had never once considered that a possibility, for I inwardly believed that only a gentleman could write with that level of excellence." He sighed and looked away again. "I confess that I have found it difficult to do such a thing as consider another perspective but given that I have no other choice *but* to accept the help of a bluestocking, I confess that I have become determined to do so."

Lydia's eyes rounded at his words, a little taken aback to hear that a gentleman, so firm and determined in his opinions, was now willing to take such a step back. "Goodness. That is... " She did not hold back her surprise. "That is an excellent thing, Your Grace. And might I say, I am grateful to you for your decision not to tell the *ton* that it was I who wrote that article."

A frown instantly tugged at the Duke's forehead. "I would never have done such a thing, Lady Lydia. I know full well that it would have caused you difficulty and I would not have brought such a thing upon you." His frown lifted just a little. "Might I also say that I have read your most recent articles and found them not only very well written but highly engaging. You write very well."

Lydia blinked in surprise. "I thank you, Your Grace." She glanced at Sophie, seeing the same astonishment in her expression also. Of all the changes in the Duke's manner, this was the most surprising though his words warmed Lydia's heart, making her settle into the Duke's company all the more as the carriage continued to make its way through London.

"It was just here, Your Grace." Lydia glanced up at him for a moment before beginning to search through the sheaves of papers. There were all manner of old circulatory papers and the like, some very dull indeed and some with only a little more interest. It took her a few minutes but she soon found it, lifting it carefully and handing it to the Duke.

He took it from her and read it, leaving Lydia to clasp her hands in front of her as she considered him. There was a muscle jumping in his jaw, a flash of anger in his eyes as he read the few short lines. It was just as she had written it in the article, though she had changed the words so that she used her own description and the like.

"It does not say who wrote this."

"It does." Standing on tiptoe, Lydia leaned against the Duke's arm as she pointed to a small signature at the very bottom. "It says that it is written by Lord R."

The Duke scowled down at the paper. "Lord R says nothing as to who it might have been. They are hiding their name, just as you did."

Lydia nodded, still scrutinizing the paper. "They are, but I do wonder if someone at the time knew who Lord R was. It might have been meant to lend credibility to his writing?" When she looked up at the Duke again, he was gazing down into her face rather than at the paper and something shifted within her. A burst of heat in her stomach, a wave of crashing awareness that she stood closer to him than she had ever been with any gentleman and that, somehow, her hand was now resting on his arm.

She stepped back, swallowed hard, and then turned away. "I am sorry if it does not bring you any answers."

"It does help a little." The Duke set the papers back down and then rubbed one hand over his face, just as Lydia turned back to face him. "I have been waiting for my mother's reply to my urgent letter, Lady Lydia. That is what prompted me to call upon you today for I received her reply only yesterday."

"Oh?" Glancing over her shoulder to make sure that Sophie was still near to her, Lydia took a small step closer to the Duke so that he could speak to her without lifting his voice too high. "Might I be so bold as to ask what she said?"

He nodded. "It was in my mind to tell you, Lady Lydia, for if you are still willing to be of aid to me, then it is imperative that you know." He let out a long sigh, his shoulders dropping a little. "My mother was forbidden to speak of the heirlooms. It was a greatly traumatizing experience for my father, for his carriage was stopped by a highwayman and he had to escape in fear for his life. The heirlooms were taken. This was back when I was only a boy, away at Eton."

"Goodness," Lydia whispered, one hand at her heart. "Then the story is true?"

With a nod, the Duke continued on. "My father's driver – Stanley – was working alongside the highwayman, it seems. The highwayman knew that he was returning from London with the heirlooms, you understand, so the driver was the one who had told him such a thing."

"But why?" Lydia asked, confused. "Why would the driver work with a highwayman? And how would they ever meet?"

"That is why my father did not say a word about the

heirlooms and why he demanded my mother remain silent," the Duke told her, lowering his head just a little as his eyes searched hers. "My father believed that someone close to him was the highwayman, though he could never prove who it was. That was why he remained silent. He did not want me to be always questioning, always looking as he had been doing. Nor did he want my opinions or thoughts of others to be clouded. Thus, all that was ever said to me was that they were lost."

"It sounds to me as though your father was a very noble gentleman," Lydia said, gently, seeing the pain that ripped through the Duke's expression. He was not looking at her, his face screwed up, heavy shadows lingering in his eyes. "He did not want you to be troubled in any way. Mayhap he believed that the heirlooms were gone and that they could not be found again."

The Duke glanced at her, then pulled his gaze away again. "Mayhap. Though I do wish he had shared his burden with me."

"I can understand that." A little hesitantly, Lydia put her hand on his arm for a brief moment – purposefully this time – and looked up into his face. "This must be troubling for you, Your Grace. I am truly sorry that I wrote as I did. If I had known it would cause you such pain, then I would never have done such a thing."

The Duke glanced at her and then, giving her a second, longer look, smiled briefly. "I know you did not mean to do so. In a way, I am grateful to you for what you discovered. I have always wondered about the heirlooms, wondered what it is that happened to them."

"And now you know."

With a slight frown pulling at his forehead, the Duke hesitated, a shadow crossing his eyes. "I think that in that, I am not certain I agree, Lady Lydia. I might now be aware of the truth of what has happened to them, certainly, but that does not mean that I know *precisely* what took place."

"But how can you know?" Lydia asked, not fully understanding what he meant. "It is so long in the past and with your father no longer here, then how can you find out the truth?"

The Duke sighed. "I do not know. But I am certain that I cannot let this rest. Indeed, it is taking a higher preference in my mind than anything else!"

This made Lydia's eyebrows lift, surprised that the Duke was now speaking so openly with her. She knew that he was come to seek a bride, for all of London were aware of that fact, and yet, here he was, stating quite plainly that what he now had on his mind were the heirlooms rather than matrimony. That was a significant thing, was it not? Though she was not quite certain what she ought to say to that.

"There is something I have not told you as yet, Lady Lydia." With a deep breath, the Duke lifted his chin a notch, his lips pressing tightly together for a moment before he spoke as if he was considering whether or not he ought to say such a thing as this. "My mother also stated in her letter that my father did, in fact, injure the highwayman. He struck him across the face though he was not certain as to where it struck."

Lydia's breath swirled in her chest as she caught her breath, her eyes rounding. "Then whoever it was will have a scar somewhere on their face!"

"Yes, exactly." There came a quick flash into the Duke's eyes as he looked at her, perhaps a little surprised with her understanding. "And if my father believed that it was someone close to him – a relative or a close friend – then I might, somehow, be able to determine who it is that now has my heirlooms." He winced. "My mother gave me four names, though I am loathe to begin settling suspicion upon any."

Lydia blinked quickly, taking in the Duke's words. "You mean to say that your father had thoughts as to who it might be that had worked alongside his driver to capture the heirlooms?"

He nodded.

"Am I permitted to ask who they are?"

A slight twist of the Duke's lips told her that her question was being considered, though mayhap he thought it a little impertinent, Lydia considered. She tipped her head, studying him, aware of just how little her dislike of him was present within her.

"You are certainly permitted to ask, Lady Lydia, though whether or not it would be wise for me to share it, I am not yet sure." A small smile touched the corner of his mouth. "Let me think on it a little more before I answer you."

Finding herself rather appreciative of his consideration and his desire to be thoughtful and careful, Lydia nodded. "But of course."

"Thank you for showing me this." His smile grew and he took a small step closer to her, leaning his head down just a little. "It seems as though I am still in need of your help, Lady Lydia. You have been able to find and discover things that I did not even know existed! It would be wise for me to ask you to continue in your desire to be of aid to me given how much success you have had thus far." His eyes caught hers, an intensity in them now. "That is, if you are still willing."

"Of course I am!" The words were given to him before she had even had time to think but Lydia was rather surprised at just how much she desired to do such a thing. "It is clear to me that this is of great sorrow to you, Your Grace. I should very much like to be of aid to you."

"I am grateful. Truly. Especially since I have not spoken well either of or to you, Lady Lydia." The Duke looked away, pushing one hand through his hair and letting it fall carelessly. "I have not thought well of bluestockings and I have made my feelings rather clear on that subject, have I not?" When Lydia nodded, he gave her a rueful smile. "You are bold enough to be honest with me, I see."

"I do not think there is any point in either pretending that it is not as you say or that it is not as severe as you have said," she answered, clearly. "Yes, you have made it plain that you think bluestockings ought to be shunned, in many ways, and that it is almost shameful for a young lady to be so."

His hazel eyes flashed though he did not immediately respond, as if he had the urge to respond a little sharply but had chosen not to. "Indeed." With a nod, he looked away. "But for you to offer me your assistance when I have spoken so says a good deal about your character, Lady Lydia, and I will not pretend that I am nothing other than grateful."

She smiled then, a gentle relief in her heart that they were no longer at odds, no longer determined to fight back against each other. Instead, there seemed to be a sense of understanding there, one that was growing steadily and that was, to her mind, quite delightful. "I value that a great deal, Your Grace. Though, if I am to help you, then I shall need to know the names of those that your father considered responsible."

It took the Duke a few moments to reply to her but when he did, it was with another heavy sigh. "And I shall, I swear to you," he answered, "but in a day or two. I must take a little more time to think on it all and discard, mayhap, a name – or more than one – that I think could not possibly have done so."

"Very well." Lydia smiled up at him, her heart lifting. "Then I look forward to speaking to you again soon, Your Grace."

The Duke tipped his head, his eyes considering as he looked back at her. It was as though he was looking at her for the very first time, as though he had seen something in her that he had not recognized before. "As do I, Lady Lydia," he answered, a genuineness to his voice that made her smile. "And I assure you, our next conversation will come very soon indeed."

CHAPTER ELEVEN

"*I* am astonished, I must say."

"And well you might be," Henry agreed with a slight shrug. "I did not ever think that I would have the agreement – nor the assistance – of a bluestocking but it seems as though I am to have it!"

Lord Kendall chuckled. "I think it very good that you shall have it. Lady Lydia appears to be a most intelligent creature and I think what she has discovered so far is evidence of her skill and her understanding. Though," he continued, with a wry smile, "I am surprised that she was so willing to offer you her aid, especially when you were so... discouraging to her efforts. Did you not state that all bluestocking ought to be spurned by society?"

Henry winced. "Yes, I did."

"And would you still hold to that?"

Henry watched as the couples danced the cotillion, letting his thoughts run over what Lord Kendall had asked. Would he still believe that a bluestocking should be shunned by society? That she ought to be looked down upon for the simple reason of desiring to learn and read and understand more than society thought she ought? More than *he* thought she ought? "I am not certain." It was the truth and though Lord Kendall snorted and said that what he had said was no true answer, Henry held to it all the same. His friend did not understand and for that, he could not blame him for he had not the same acquaintance with Lady Lydia and did not understand the influence she had upon him. He had wanted to say that yes, bluestockings were the sort of creature that should be pushed away from society so that *other* young ladies did not have the same notions and ideas as they but at the very same time, now admitted that one bluestocking, at least, had been of great aid to him personally – and that had come about solely because of her learning, her reading and her desire to further it all. Could he really state that such a thing ought to be seen as less than desirable, especially when she was willing to assist him in his search for the truth?

"You hesitate!" Lord Kendall chuckled, a grin spreading right across his face. "Then you must be reconsidering!"

"I am not certain of what I think," Henry answered, truthfully. "I am not sure I can have the same position as I once did given that she has not only clear talent when it comes to writing those articles, and also because, despite my poor remarks, has suggested that she might be of aid to me." He watched as Lord Kendall's eyebrows lifted. "Indeed. She is remarkable in that way, I must say."

"So it seems." Lord Kendall's eyebrows rose all the higher as he studied Henry's face, though Henry did not know what it was his friend searched for. "Now, might I ask what your thinking is about Lady Judith?"

Letting out a snort, Henry rolled his eyes and went to sip his punch rather than answer.

"Oh?" Lord Kendall looked and sounded surprised. "I

thought you considered her to be in excellent standing given your list of requirements."

"Alas," Henry answered, with a wry smile, "one of those requirements is that she cannot have a great interest in another gentleman. And in that regard, it is quite clear to me that Lady Judith has no desire to be in my company."

A twinkle came into Lord Kendall's eye, though he said nothing.

"I can see that you wish to laugh but I do appreciate your willingness to hold it back," Henry continued, with a rueful chuckle of his own. "Yes, I did not imagine for a moment that a young lady might consider a gentleman with a lower title over myself, but it appears that Lord Telford holds Lady Judith's interest more than I."

"I see." Lord Kendall schooled his face into a calm expression though the glint in his eye did not leave. "Mayhap you have not considered how finding and securing a young lady's attentions might be a little more difficult than expected? That is a trial in itself!"

"So it would seem."

"Though you cannot give up! Lady Ann might be a wise consideration, yes?"

Henry sighed. "I am not sure that I wish to pursue that particular lady at present. In fact, I am not certain I wish to pursue *any* young lady at this moment! My thoughts are centered solely on the heirlooms."

"And that is to your detriment!" Lord Kendall exclaimed. "There are many young ladies who are ready and waiting for you to catch their eye! You can think and search on your heirlooms, of course, but you can also surely consider your future and any match you might make, can you not?"

"I – I am not sure." Henry scowled, rubbing one hand

over his eyes. "It is a heavy weight upon my heart – the heirlooms, I mean – and that seems to be taking up a good deal of my thinking and my time." Ever since he had received the letter from his mother, Henry had to admit that he had done nothing but think on it and the names therein. "Yes, it would be a distraction, I suppose, but – "

"Then pursue both!" Lord Kendall exclaimed. "You do yourself a disservice if you do not."

With a slow nod, Henry told himself that his friend was quite correct. He *could* do both. In fact, it might be good for him to pursue both matters at once, for then he would not think about the heirlooms so much and could distract himself with the consideration of young ladies instead!

"Lady Ann is present this evening," Lord Kendall continued, perhaps aware of Henry's thoughts. "I am sure that if you asked her to dance, she would accept you." He chuckled. "Any young lady would accept you, I am sure, but what I mean to say is that she would accept with delight."

"I should go and find her," Henry agreed, his eyes now searching the crowd. "You are right, Kendall. My thoughts have been heavy of late – to the point that I quite ruined my visit to Lady Judith which, no doubt made her think all the lesser of me!" He winced as his friend laughed, though a grin spread across his face all the same. "I shall take my leave of you."

"Oh, I shall join you, I think!" Lord Kendall answered, with another laugh. "My friend, you do not seem to understand just how many young ladies are eager for your company! And if I am beside you, then I shall have the chance to take the dance cards from the most eligible, the most beautiful, and the genteel young ladies in all of London – and who knows? I might then end up falling quite in love with one of them."

This made Henry chuckle and, setting his glass down, he made his way with his friend into the crowd. He could not help but notice the many glances that came his way, seeing how many of the young ladies began to whisper to one another, how some batted their eyelashes at him and smiled in delight at his brief consideration of them, though Henry did not take too much notice. There were many young debutantes in London, that he knew, but he was entirely uncertain as to whether any of them would be suitable. Thus far, he only knew that there were many who were bold enough to smile in such a way at him while others whispered to others though that he considered a little indelicate. Perhaps Lord Kendall was quite correct, perhaps this in itself was a difficulty enough! To secure one young lady's attention – a young lady who matched all that he desired – might not be as easy as he had once considered.

"There, I can see her. She is standing alongside Lady Miriam whom, I might add, is not someone that I would appreciate you considering."

"Oh?" Henry grinned at his friend. "Is she someone that you have in mind?"

Lord Kendall shrugged nonchalantly. "I have noticed her, that is all."

Henry made to say more, wanting to rib his friend but they were now much too close to the ladies for him to do so. He bowed in greeting, only to notice, as his head lifted, that Lady Lydia was standing next to Lady Ann on the other side. Having been caught up in observing Lady Miriam – who was quite beautiful with her golden tresses and vivid blue eyes – he had not even glanced towards the other ladies present. His heart lurched in a most unexpected way though he made certain that his expression remained quite calm.

"Good evening, Lady Ann, Lady Lydia." Glancing towards Lord Kendall who was doing nothing other than smiling at Lady Miriam, Henry nudged him lightly. "Might you perhaps make the introductions, my friend?"

Lord Kendall flushed and quickly obliged though Henry himself found himself quite caught by the smile on Lady Lydia's face. It was warm and filled with delight as she observed Lord Kendall and Lady Miriam. Was she aware of Lord Kendall's interest in the lady or was it just that he had made himself far too obvious in his manner and in the color of his face? Henry found himself smiling at Lady Lydia's obvious pleasure, noticing the way that her green eyes seemed to dance with delight.

"We have come in the hope that you three ladies will not have had every dance taken thus far," Lord Kendall continued, as Henry nodded quickly, drawing his attention away from Lady Lydia. "Alas, the Duke realized a little too late that he wished to dance and thus, we came in search of any willing ladies to stand up with us!"

"Then you will find us most obliging," Lady Miriam answered though, Henry noticed, she was looking solely to Lord Kendall when she spoke. "I certainly have some dances remaining."

"And you, Lady Ann?" Remembering that he was to direct his attention towards Lady Ann, Henry smiled at her warmly. "I do hope that you have some dances remaining?" He took the dance card from Lady Miriam as he spoke, scribbling his name down for the cotillion and then handing it back to her, looking still expectantly at Lady Ann.

"You are very kind to ask, Your Grace," came her response, as Lord Kendall lingered over Lady Miriam's dance card. "I would be very glad to give you my dance card, of course."

She did so with seeming eagerness and Henry took it, looking to see what dances might still be available. The waltz was already taken and for that, he was grateful. It meant that he would not have to disappoint her by choosing *not* to take the dance, while at the same time, feeling no pressure to set his name to it in the first place. Settling for the country dance, he handed her back the dance card and took the lady in, seeing the gentle blush on her cheeks and smiling at the way her eyes darted to the card, only for her to smile. Clearly, he had chosen well.

"I do so love the country dance," she told him, looking back into his face. "And thus far, no one had taken it! You cannot know of my delight, Your Grace."

Silently thinking to himself that Lady Ann was more than pleasing in her manner, Henry inclined his head just a little, never taking his eyes from hers. "I am looking forward to the dance already, Lady Ann!" Finding himself quickly drawn into conversation, Henry spoke on all manner of topics, speaking about his estate, finding her eager to learn all that she could about him. Lady Miriam too spoke with them, telling Henry a little more about Lady Ann; her good nature, and her love of the garden. Henry smiled, nodded, and listened with eagerness, only for a sudden thought to strike him, hard.

Where is Lady Lydia?

A hand grasped at his heart, squeezing it hard as he realized that not only had he missed out on the opportunity to ask her for her dance card, but he had forgotten about her entirely! He had not meant to do such a thing, had not meant to leave her out of the conversation but somehow, he had been so caught up with Lady Ann and his thoughts towards her that he had managed to do that very thing. His heart racing, he looked this way and that, quickly forgetting the conversation with Lady Ann, Lady Miriam, and Lord Kendall and eager instead, now to find the lady and to apologize profusely.

"Is something the matter, Your Grace?"

Henry turned his head back towards Lady Ann, nodding as he did so. "Yes, there is. I appear to have quite forgotten about Lady Lydia! She was here only a few moments ago and I did mean to ask her for her dance card but now it seems, I have lost the opportunity."

Lady Ann laughed and waved one hand as if to dismiss his concerns. "Oh, Your Grace, you need not think such thoughts about Lady Lydia! I am sure she will not mind in the least. She does not appear to be in the least bit concerned about dancing."

Henry blinked, then let a frown settle over his expression. "All the same, I should like to make certain she does not feel as though she has been abandoned."

At this, Lady Ann let out another trill of a laugh as though what he had said was rather ridiculous, and heat began to spiral in Henry's chest. "Your Grace, you are *much* too concerned when you need not be! She will think nothing of it, for I am quite sure that she has no interest in any gentleman present – and very few gentlemen will be interested in her either!"

"What do you mean by that?" Henry asked quickly, catching the way that Lord Kendall frowned though, Henry thought, it was not because of what he had asked but rather from what Lady Ann had said. "Is not every debutante here to catch the attention of a gentleman?"

Lady Ann glanced at Lady Miriam, let out a giggle – one that Lady Miriam did not join in with – and then looked back to Henry. "Your Grace, I should not speak out of turn but I shall tell you this so that you do not concern yourself any longer." She came a little closer to him, a hint of lavender swirling around him as her eyes lifted to his. "Lady Lydia is too much of a bluestocking for any of the gentlemen in London to consider, I am sure! She has tried to hide it but I know she cannot! Do you know, I heard her in deep conversation with Lord Wilcher over his plans for the improvement of his estate? It appears that she knows something about the architecture from the continent which, apparently, is being brought to England's shores also!" She giggled again but Henry's frown only sank deeper. "It seems to me that Lady Lydia knows a good deal more than a young lady ought, and no gentleman will want a bride who understands more than they!"

Henry swallowed hard, aware that his first instinct was to agree with Lady Ann but that, soon after that, came the desire to argue *against* it. Lady Lydia had shown herself to be a competent young lady and though he was still becoming accustomed to the idea of being in company with a bluestocking, Henry did not feel himself eager to mock Lady Lydia, as he might once have done. Indeed, the more he considered it, the more he found Lady Ann to be the one lacking instead of Lady Lydia herself.

"You will have to excuse me," he said, a trifle brusquely as he stepped back from Lady Ann, choosing to say nothing about what she had said but instead, keep his thoughts entirely to himself. "Regardless of what you have said, Lady Ann, I do feel it my obligation to go in search of Lady Lydia to make certain all is well."

"Oh." Lady Ann began to blink quickly, her eyes searching his. "I quite understand." Her smile began to fade, a paleness coming into her cheeks. "Forgive me, I did not mean to speak in any disparaging way, I only sought to assuage your conscience."

"And you have done so," Henry answered, bowing quickly. "Though I must do what I feel is my duty. Good evening, Lady Ann, Lady Miriam. I shall seek you out again at the time of our dance."

Without another word, he made his way from them both, his heart pounding as worry began to gnaw at the edge of his mind. Lady Ann's words haunted him, sounding a good deal more callous now even though he recognized that, only a few days ago, he would have agreed wholeheartedly!

She has changed me, he thought to himself, searching for Lady Lydia with every step he took. *And I cannot think it a bad thing.*

CHAPTER TWELVE

*L*ydia smiled as the Duke of Melrose and Lord Kendall took the dance cards from Lady Miriam and then Lady Ann. She had noticed the interest that came into Lord Kendall's expression when he had first set eyes on Lady Miriam, though she knew they were already acquainted. It was of great interest to her to see that he was almost entirely focused upon her, his every look and every word given to Lady Miriam – to the point that the Duke of Melrose had been forced to ask him to make the introductions! She did not know Lady Miriam particularly well but she had heard that Lord Kendall was an excellent gentleman and the little time she had spent in his company had only confirmed that.

Bringing her hands together, Lydia slowly slid the silk ribbon from her wrist, fully prepared to give the Duke her dance card the moment he asked. Lord Kendall too, of course, for the gentlemen would not be as improper as to ignore her! Given that they had asked for Lady Ann's and Lady Miriam's, she was certain she would be next. Her heart leaped at the thought of being led out for two dances by not one but two distinguished gentlemen, a little surprised that she did not feel any hesitation when it came to dancing with the Duke! After their last conversation, she had not felt any dislike or any lingering upset. Instead, there had been a sense of relief – almost gladness – that there was to be no tension or the like between them any longer. She saw a value in his consideration of her, happy to know that he was, at the very least, reconsidering his opinion as regarded bluestockings. To acknowledge aloud that he would be grateful for her aid and assistance as he tried to find the truth about the heirlooms had made her heart happy and it had remained so even until this very moment.

She watched as the Duke handed back Lady Ann's dance card, preparing now for him to turn his attention towards her.

"I do so love the country dance and thus far, no one had taken it! You cannot know of my delight, Your Grace." Lady Ann smiled warmly at the Duke and Lydia licked her lips, hoping that he would soon remember to look towards her. The Duke inclined his head just a little, his eyes fixing to Lady Ann.

"I am looking forward to the dance already, Lady Ann!"

Lady Ann beamed at the Duke, turning her body just a little so that Lydia was effectively pushed back from the group.

Her heart began to sink as the Duke laughed at something Lady Ann said, realizing now that Lady Ann was deliberately attempting to secure the Duke's attention solely for herself. Whilst Lydia was fully aware that it was precisely what every young lady might be expected to do given that it was the Duke that they spoke with, she could not help but feel the sting nonetheless.

She blinked, a little surprised to feel tears behind her

eyes as the Duke leaned closer to Lady Ann, evidently appearing to forget that she had been present also. Lydia did not want to blame Lord Kendall for he was standing next to the Duke and further away from her and, given the way he was more than a little interested in Lady Miriam, it was easy enough to understand why he might forget she was present.

But the Duke?

Lydia blinked rapidly again, turning around and making her way from the small group, feeling as though she were slowly shrinking in stature. There was a heaviness in her heart that she could not fully explain, a sense that somehow, she was more than a little lesser than the other young ladies. Lady Ann had been a trifle spiteful in how she had responded in trying to pull the Duke away, that much was clear, but for the Duke to have been so easily pulled aside meant that, to Lydia's mind, it was clear she was of no particular interest.

But do I want to be? Lydia frowned as she made her way to the side of the ballroom, choosing to hide in the shadows instead of going in search of her mother or Lady Markham. For the time being, she wanted to be alone, wanted to be entirely in solitude so she might work through her thoughts and feelings before returning to the ball. She had some dances still remaining to dance and she could not stand up with either gentleman when her mind was in such confusion, for she would make a dreadful dance partner, and thereafter, her mother would berate her dreadfully!

Why did it matter to her if the Duke did not think of her? Why should she give any consideration to the fact that he had turned away from her and forgotten that she too had a dance card? She had agreed to support him, to help him in his search for the heirlooms but that did not mean that their acquaintance had any special significance! Yes, it meant a great deal that he had not rejected her, given that she was a bluestocking, but she could not permit herself to think that this was the reason he had chosen to ignore her.

Could she?

Her brow furrowed hard as she bit her lip. Could it be that the Duke of Melrose had chosen not to stand up with her, had chosen to deliberately forget her dance card because she was a bluestocking and he could not be seen to dance with her in the midst of a society ball? The heat behind her eyes rose again to a terrible strength and she was forced to blink furiously to push them away.

"And who is it we have hiding here?"

Lydia lifted her head, a little surprised to see a gentleman coming to join her. Panic gripped at her heart as she stepped back from him, suddenly afraid that he had somewhat nefarious intentions. "I – I do not think – "

"Now, you do not need to look so afraid." The gentleman smiled and swept into a bow. "I have seen you in company with my nephew recently, have I not?"

"Your nephew?" Lydia did not know of whom he spoke, taking in the grey-haired gentleman and trying to see any sort of likeness to the gentlemen in her acquaintance. "I confess, I do not know who it is you speak of."

The gentleman chuckled. "Forgive me, I have not introduced myself. It is not the proper thing to do, I suppose, but you shall have to permit me." He inclined his head. "I am the Earl of Chesterfield. My nephew is the Duke of Melrose and I am certain I saw you in his company very lately, did I not?"

"Oh!" Lydia smiled with relief, glad now that this

gentleman did not mean anything improper. "Yes, I am acquainted with the Duke of Melrose. Lady Markham and I accompanied him recently to the library, you might have seen us in the carriage then?"

The gentleman nodded. "Yes, that is it precisely. I confess I could not easily forget a lady with hair the color of the sunset!"

Lydia flushed, hopeful that this was meant as a compliment.

"And where is my nephew this evening, I wonder?" the gentleman continued, turning to look all about him. "Is he present this evening, do you know? He and I have only managed one conversation and as yet, I have not even managed to call to take tea! Is that not quite dreadful!" He grinned as he spoke and made Lydia smile along with him.

"I was speaking with him only a few minutes ago," Lydia answered, gesturing to her left. "He was just over there."

As the gentleman turned his head in the direction she pointed in, Lydia was caught by what her eyes took in. Lord Chesterfield had a small scar that ran just along one side of his cheek towards his eye.

Could it be...?

She shook her head to herself, just as Lord Chesterfield turned his attention back towards her. If this was the Duke's uncle, then he would, no doubt, have seen him over many years and would know precisely what that scar came from. Besides which, she could not even be sure whether or not this gentleman was on the list of the four names that the Duke had been given!

"My own two children are already wed and settled," the Earl continued, as Lydia smiled quickly. "I come to London at the sole behest of my wife, I confess! If it were for myself, then I would stay at my estate these summer months!"

Lydia smiled and tilted her head. "Do you have a large estate? I have been reading recently about the idea of crop rotation and confess to having found it a most interesting subject."

The surprise that leaped into Lord Chesterfield's expression was instant and Lydia quickly dropped her head, a flush of embarrassment creeping up into her face. She had, inadvertently so, spoken of something that a young lady such as herself ought not to know anything about. Yet again, she had given herself away.

"Crop rotation, eh?" Lord Chesterfield's voice held a note of interest. "I have heard of it but I have not considered it as yet, I confess."

Lydia glanced up but chose to say nothing more. She did not want to make herself more obvious for that would bring nothing but trouble to her.

"Ah, there you are!"

Her heart leaped up furiously as none other than the Duke of Melrose came towards them both, coming to stand beside his uncle and looking at him in surprise. "Chesterfield, good evening!"

"Good evening, nephew." Lord Chesterfield set one hand on the Duke's shoulder. "I have just been speaking with this *very* fine young lady whom I saw in company with you recently. On a carriage ride to the library, I believe?"

The Duke nodded, though his gaze caught Lydia's, his eyes searching hers though Lydia did not know the answer to the question that was settling there.

"Lydia, I was just – oh!"

Lydia's face grew hot as her mother came to stand directly beside her, only for her eyebrows to lift in surprise as she looked to the Duke of Melrose and then to Lord Chesterfield. "Mama, I was just speaking with the Earl of Chesterfield. I was coming in search of you when – "

"When I interrupted," Lord Chesterfield said, warmly, turning to bow low towards Lady Hampshire. "Goodness, what a marvel your daughter is!"

A flicker came into Lady Hampshire's eye and Lydia's stomach twisted. What was the Earl going to say now? Was it going to be something that would bring Lydia nothing but upset and anger once they were alone?

"I quite agree." The Duke spoke now before either Lady Hampshire could ask what was meant by such a statement or Lord Chesterfield could say more. "In fact, I also came to interrupt the conversation, which I had not yet apologized for." He cleared his throat briefly and then bowed his head. "Forgive me for breaking into your conversation with my uncle, Lady Lydia. I had come in the hope of speaking to you for a moment."

"You wish to speak with my daughter?" Lady Hampshire's voice was a little quiet, perhaps a little overcome with surprise. "I am sure she would oblige you, Your Grace."

Lydia threw her mother a sharp look, wishing that she could wipe out any hope that her mother had of Lydia being pulled into a close acquaintance with the Duke. Whatever it was he wanted to say, Lydia was sure it did not hold any real significance.

The Duke nodded and smiled briefly though there was a slight flare of light in his eyes, a light which Lydia could not quite understand. Was it relief? Or something more?

"If you might, Lady Lydia?" The Duke gestured to his left and Lydia, with a nod to Lord Chesterfield and another look to her mother, stepped away from them and towards him. They did not move very far away, however, only a few steps so that her mother could keep her in sight but also so that the Duke might be able to speak freely.

"Lady Lydia." The Duke turned to her, rubbing one hand over his chin as his eyes darted here and there rather than looking at her. "I did not mean – that is, I understand that I *did* but it was not my intention to do so."

Confused, she frowned. "I am afraid that I do not know what it is that you mean, Your Grace."

"Your dance card. The conversation." He flung out one hand in the vague direction where he had come from. "I was speaking with Lady Ann, Lady Miriam, and yourself but though I signed *their* dance cards, I did not sign yours. You disappeared before I could do so!"

Lydia lifted one eyebrow just a little. "And you did not seem to even notice that I was present, Your Grace." She held up one hand as he began to protest. "I do not mind in the least bit if you are intrigued by Lady Ann, Your Grace," she continued, ignoring the slight twist of her heart as she spoke, "but to be forgotten is not a situation that I had a desire to linger in. Thus, I took my leave." She lifted her shoulders just a little, fully aware that she was pretending that she did not feel all that she truly *had* felt when he had turned away from her. "You did not need to trouble yourself."

"Oh, but I had to." The fervency in his voice surprised her. "I had no other choice but to come after you, for I felt myself so ashamed of my lack of awareness, I could not leave it as it stood. I did not want you to feel any injury – or if you already had, as I believe you must do, then I would do all that I could to apologize for it. Which I am doing now." He inclined his head. "I humbly apologize for my lack of awareness and consideration, Lady Lydia. It was not in the least bit purposeful."

Lydia swallowed at the knot which had formed in her throat. "Then it was not because you did not wish to dance with me?" Her cheeks grew hot as his eyes shot to hers, having had no intention of speaking so and yet finding that her heart had put words in her mouth before she had been able to prevent it.

"No, not in the least." The Duke came a fraction closer to her, his gaze searching hers. "I did not do so deliberately, I assure you." His gaze grew gentle. "Did you truly think that I would do so?"

She nodded. "Yes, I did."

"Because you are a bluestocking?"

Again, she nodded. "Precisely. I know that you have accepted my help and in that, our connection can be strong and assured. However, in society and for dancing and the like, you might well desire to step away from me, aware that there are those in society who are already aware of my tendency towards bluestocking ways." She dropped her head and pulled her gaze away. "I can understand that. You are a Duke after all."

Much to her relief, he shook his head. "No, not in the least. That does not affect my situation at all or my thinking. I would be more than glad to have you stand up with me for at least one of the dances. Would you be willing to give me your dance card? I should like to see if there is even one dance I might be able to take!"

Lydia, aware that she had only a few names on her dance card, flushed. "I am afraid it will not be as full as Lady Ann's, Your Grace."

"That does not matter in the least, I assure you."

With a tightness in her chest still, Lydia took her dance card from her wrist and, a trifle reluctantly still, handed it to the Duke. Their fingers touched for just a moment and a streak of heat rushed up her arm and into her chest, making her heart quicken. The Duke did not look down at the dance card either, holding her gaze for a long moment as though there was something that he too had felt but did not fully understand.

Then, he dropped his gaze and looked at her card. Lydia clasped her hands tightly together and looked away, wondering why it was that she felt such a strange tension twisting through her, why she had this panic gripping her heart as though somehow, she was almost excited by what the Duke was going to offer her.

I must talk to him about his uncle also.

"There." The Duke smiled and handed her back her dance card. "I hope that will be enough to prove to you that there is nothing about you that holds me back from dancing with you."

Lydia's heart thundered furiously as she looked down to see his name written for the waltz. In an instant, she could not breathe, her heart squeezing, her stomach roiling as she tried to take in the significance of this moment.

I am to be dancing the waltz with the Duke!

"Are you quite sure?"

He chuckled and nodded. "Yes, I am quite certain. I know that there may be a few lifted eyebrows and some might be a little surprised that I have chosen even to *dance* the waltz given that I have not done so thus far, but I think it is quite right and fitting for me to do so." Smiling still, he leaned a little closer to her. "So long as *you* are contented?"

"Yes, of course I am," she breathed, looking down at her dance card again as though to make sure that she had not misread what he had written. "Thank you, Your Grace."

"I am glad to have been able to rectify my mistake."

With a nod, he turned his head and made to step away. "Excuse me, I shall let you return to your mother now."

"Wait." Her hand snaked out and caught his though she let it go again as if it had burned her skin. "Forgive me, Your Grace, I wanted to speak with you about your uncle."

Thankfully, he smiled, showing no frustration or irritation whatsoever. "What about him?"

Lydia hesitated, licking her lips as she considered how she was to mention to the Duke about the scar she had seen on his face. "I know that you have not yet shared with me the list of the four names that your mother suggested," she began, speaking slowly and with great care so that the words she chose were all quite suitable. "I did wonder if your uncle might be on that list?"

This made the Duke's smile fade in an instant. "I beg your pardon?"

She swallowed hard. "Was your uncle's name on the list from your father?"

Slowly, the Duke nodded. "Yes, in fact. It was."

"I have noticed that he has a scar on his face," Lydia continued, though she moved closer to him and kept her voice low as she spoke. "I did wonder if... "

The Duke's eyes flared though he did not respond to her immediately. It took him some moments to reply, appearing to need to compose himself before he said anything.

"I have no close connection with my uncle," he said, eventually. "I do not know him well. Thus, I would have not noticed any such thing on his appearance – or if I had, then I would not have connected it to my heirlooms! Thank you for informing me, Lady Lydia. Mayhap... " Hesitating, he looked away and then turned his gaze back to her again. "Might you like to take a walk with me in the park tomorrow? There is more than I would like to share with you."

She nodded, relieved that he had not responded badly to her. "I should like that very much, Your Grace."

"Then I look forward to tomorrow – and to our dance later this evening." With a smile, he inclined his head. "Good evening, Lady Lydia."

CHAPTER THIRTEEN

"Did you find your dance... pleasing?"

Henry rolled his eyes as Lord Kendall grinned at him. "You are not in the least bit vague, are you?"

"No, I am not. I find that being direct is usually the best course of action." Lord Kendall chuckled as they waited by the carriage for Lady Lydia to arrive. "You have not danced the waltz before, have you? I have heard many in the *ton* say so and that was only last evening!"

"Yes, yes." Henry rolled his eyes. "I danced the waltz with Lady Lydia and I am glad that I did so! She was clearly upset at my stepping away from her – ignoring her, frankly – and what she asked me did strike at my heart." Seeing his friend's questioning look, Henry smiled briefly. "It was evident that she believed I had chosen to forget about her deliberately, so that I would not have to dance with a bluestocking. I wanted to assure her that it was not so and thus, rather than choose the cotillion or some such thing, I chose the waltz."

Lord Kendall's expression brightened. "Then I think very well of you for doing so, my friend. I hope you made your point? She appeared to be quite delighted when she was dancing with you."

Henry's heart filled with a warmth that he had experienced only once before – when he had been dancing with Lady Lydia the previous evening. It had been both a strange and a wonderful experience, for he had not only found himself delighted at being able to have her as a dance partner, but he had also discovered a fresh sense of wonder in taking her into his arms. It was as if he had never danced the waltz before, as though he had never even *stepped* into a room with young ladies before. It filled every part of his being with happiness, making him feel as if he were practically glowing from within. They had barely said a word to one another as they had danced, but Henry had been entirely unable to look away from her. When, he had wondered, had he first realized just how beautiful the lady was? It had been something of a revelation for he saw then, for the very first time, that he was not regarding her with any sort of dislike or contempt, as he had done before. Yes, she was a bluestocking and yes, he had found that type of young lady most disagreeable in the past but now... now, there was something different.

"My friend?"

Realizing that he had been lost in his thoughts about the lady, Henry flushed and shrugged. "Yes. Lady Lydia was very pleased with our dance."

"As were you, I think."

Henry was spared from having to answer the question for, at that very moment, Lady Lydia stepped down from a carriage nearby, swiftly followed by her mother. Henry smiled at the first, only to see the beam of delight that had spread across Lady Hampshire's expression. Clearly, she thought that this was a mark of interest upon her daughter, though Henry intended it to be nothing of the sort! His stomach twisted, suddenly concerned that Lady Hampshire would soon spread news of his walk with her daughter all through society... but then, he supposed, nothing could be done for that. If he wanted Lady Lydia's company and her aid – which he did – then that would mean speaking with her at length. Which was precisely what he intended to do.

"Good afternoon." Putting a smile on his face, Henry made his way towards Lady Lydia, greeting first her and then her mother. "Thank you for joining me, Lady Lydia. And for your attendance also, Lady Hampshire."

"Oh, but of course!" Lady Hampshire put one hand on his arm for just a moment, her eyes dancing with clear hope and expectation. "I shall be a short distance away as you walk. I am sure you understand."

"I do." With a smile still on his face, Henry turned to Lady Lydia, a little surprised at how much his heart leaped when her eyes met his. They were like emeralds, glittering gently as she smiled at him. "How excellent to see you, Lady Lydia. Are you quite ready to walk with me?"

"I am." She accepted his arm and they turned to walk together into the park, the sunshine beaming down around them. With a lightness in his step and a joy in his heart – a joy that he could not quite explain – Henry walked with her for a time in silence, simply enjoying being in her company. Lady Lydia too seemed quite contented, for every so often, she would glance up at him, smile, and then look away again.

"I did enjoy our dance last evening," Henry began, as she looked up at him again. "I know there will have been some remarks made to you but I hope that there have been none that are at all distressing."

Much to his surprise, she laughed softly at this, her

expression lighting up with a fresh brightness. "Good gracious, no!" she exclaimed, as Henry found himself smiling. "I am not in the least bit concerned about anyone who might have something to say about me. Rather, the only thing that troubles me is whether or not anyone else discovers that I am a bluestocking and that is only because of the trouble that would fall on me because of my parents' dislike of such a thing!"

"Then I am contented," Henry told her, aware that his sense of happiness in her company was growing each time they met. "Mayhap we shall have the opportunity to dance again soon?"

"I should like that." Her smile was warm and genuine and Henry's whole being seemed to fill with a fresh warmth that ran right through him. The sun was high, the breeze light and gentle and his company, quite perfect.

Though she is a bluestocking, came the gentle reminder as he looked away from her. *And you cannot ever tie yourself to her.*

Henry cleared his throat at this, a little concerned that, somehow, she had heard his thoughts. Why was he thinking such a thing? It was not as though he was overly drawn to the lady, not as if he were thinking of her as a potential bride... was it?

"What was it you wished to speak to me about, Your Grace?"

Blinking, Henry pushed away his present thoughts and tried to recall why he had asked her to walk with him. "Ah, yes." With a glance in her direction, he thought about how to begin. "I wanted to share with you the four names that my father had told my mother about. The gentlemen that he considered might be responsible for the theft of his heirlooms."

"Oh yes! I should be glad to know and, truth be told, honored that you would be willing to share them with me. I too have been thinking about how one might discover the perpetrator and I think I have a few suggestions for you, though it will depend on what you share with me, of course."

Hearing the flicker of interest in her voice, Henry reminded himself, yet again, of just how fortunate he was to have such a person beside him. She had offered her support and was now giving it to him willingly, thinking through all that had been said to her previously and considering what she might do next to be of aid to him. That was a rare thing indeed and Henry was grateful for it – for even Lord Kendall had never offered such a thing! Though given the way he was caught up with Lady Miriam, Henry could not hold that against him.

"I thank you for your willingness to be of assistance to me," he began, remembering the names with clarity. "One of them, as you suggested, was my uncle, Lord Chesterfield. There is also Lord Dunford, who was very close friends with my father, another by the name of Lord Northstone, though he has, sadly, passed away. Then the final name was one Lord Montrose. Again, he was closely connected to my father and I think also may be vaguely related to us."

"I see." Lady Lydia looked up at him. "I presume you are unable to find out anything from Lord Northstone's family?"

Henry shook his head. "I do not think I can at present. They are all still in mourning, you understand. Besides which, they live very far from both London and from my estate, so any enquiries would have to be done over letter and that might prove difficult."

"So," she continued, with a nod, "we then have your

uncle, Lord Dunford, who is a gentleman I am already acquainted with, and Lord Montrose." She glanced up at him, a question in her eyes, and, seeing it, Henry felt he knew what it was she wanted to say.

"I have done nothing by way of enquiry," he said, as she nodded slowly, her gaze darting away from his. "I have only been considering what it is I must do."

"And have you any thoughts? Any intentions or plan?"

Henry winced. "No, I have not. Not as yet. In truth, Lydia, my heart and mind have been so troubled with a great many thoughts that I have not known where to go."

For whatever reason, Lady Lydia had slowed her steps and Henry frowned, glancing towards her, only to see surprise in her expression. It took him a few moments to realize that he had called her 'Lydia' instead of her formal title – something only reserved for close acquaintances. He opened his mouth to apologize, only to frown again. Their acquaintance had not been overly long but there was something about her that made him feel very close to her indeed. Whether it was that there was now an openness in their connection that he had come to appreciate or the fact that she had been nothing but clear with him about who she was, without any pretense or the like, Henry could not say but whatever it was, it made him feel as though he did not need to be as formal with her as before. With a soft smile, he lifted his shoulders. "If it is just to be you and I, you are more than welcome to refer to me as 'Melrose', should you wish it. After all, we have spoken of so much and you know a great deal about my family and the like! We have become rather close in a short space of time, have we not?"

It took her a few seconds to respond but when she did, it was with a most brilliant smile that made her eyes sparkle and her cheeks flush gently. Henry's breath hitched, stunned by her sudden beauty. His mouth went dry as his stomach swirled, aware that this feeling, this desire to be closer to her, had nothing to do with her willingness to aid him. Instead, it came from a genuine interest in her, an attraction that was pulling him ever closer to her.

But she does not fulfill my requirements!

"You are most generous, Your Grace... I mean, Melrose." Lady Lydia ducked her head as she spoke, her face red now. "Thank you. I will be glad to do so when we are just you and I." She paused, then continued. "I have been thinking about what we might do and in truth, I think it may be fairly simple."

"Oh?" Henry tried to dismiss his feelings, tried to push away his new awareness but felt it cling tight to him, despite his silent demands for it to release him. "What do you think we should do?"

Lady Lydia smiled up at him, a confidence in her eyes and in her expression. "In the articles I have been writing, I have been able to find out a good deal about every family that I chose to consider. Can I not then simply do the same as I have been doing for these gentlemen? I shall research their family, the area that they live in, and the like."

A trifle confused, Henry frowned. "What will that achieve?"

A quiet laugh broke from her lips. "Forgive me for my lack of explanation. It will show us which, if any, were once impoverished. And if their fortunes suddenly improved."

"Around the time – or after the time – that my father's heirlooms were taken," Henry breathed, a clarity coming over him in an instant and stealing his breath. He stopped walking, turned to look down at Lady Lydia, and found himself lost for words. In a single instant, she had offered him a solution for what he had been fighting to find out for so long. He had never even considered why the heirlooms would have been stolen but she, with her clear thinking and good sense, had understood that the main reason someone would do so would be to secure their own fortune. And in recognizing that, she had come to an understanding of what needed to happen to secure the perpetrator.

"Might I suggest that, once we have that information, you might approach whoever it is and mention the name of your father's driver? I think their reaction would tell you whether the conclusion we have reached is correct."

"Of course, of *course*," Henry answered, fervently as he reached out both hands to capture her two. "I shall also look for a scar." Looking down into her eyes, Henry shook his head, overwhelmed by just how wonderful a lady he had found. "My dear Lydia, you are truly remarkable."

This made her eyebrows lift just a little, though a small, gentle smile touched the corners of her mouth.

"I mean every word of it," he continued, feeling as though all he had ever thought about bluestockings – even his lingering concerns that he had thought of only a few minutes ago – shattering completely. "Lydia, you have thought of the solution needed to find the person responsible!"

"That is only *if* it is one of the names that your father considered," she answered, a slight warning in her voice. "It may not be."

With a small shake of his head, Henry gripped her hands, harder. "No, I am certain that my father will have thought correctly. He will have given great consideration to it and that is why he wanted to keep it a secret from me." Blowing out a long breath, he held her gaze. "Are you certain you are willing to do such a thing for me? To search through all of your books and papers to find out what you can about these three men?"

She nodded. "Of course. I know where to look and I know what sources to search for. I am sure that you will have some books and documents also, however?"

Henry nodded. "Indeed."

"It will not take me more than a sennight, I think," she continued, as Henry's eyes widened, marveling at her ability and her determination. "I shall have the information for you within that time, Melrose."

Speechless, it took Henry some time to think of what to say in response. All he did at that time was keep her hands in his and his eyes locked to hers. Had he the same thoughts as she? Had he had any real thoughts as to what it was he might do by way of discovering who it was that had taken his father's heirlooms? No, he had not, and yet, here she was with this simple, easy consideration as to what he might do by way of discovering it. It was not only astonishing, it was more than a little remarkable and he found himself quite charmed by her.

"You are utterly astonishing."

Those words did not make her smile though Henry quickly pressed her hands, wanting her to know that he meant those words to bring her nothing but good.

"You are *astonishing*," he said again, more emphatically this time. "I do not think that I know any gentleman of my acquaintance who would even *think* as quickly as you have done! You have made not only deliberations but brought an idea to me that will bring me the clarity I have longed for. A longing which I have held to my heart for many a year."

She smiled then, a touch of pink on her cheeks. "I thank you for the compliment. It seems to me as though you appreciate bluestockings a little more than you have done before now?"

This made him chuckle, seeing the glint in her eye. "Yes, indeed. I think that my thoughts about bluestockings have been quite thrown about! I have no choice but to think well of them given that I have you as an example." Reluctantly, he released her hands. "You have offered me more than I deserve, Lydia. Do not think that I am unaware of that."

Her smile gentled as she held his gaze. "I think we have stumbled into something of a friendship, have we not?"

Or something more.

The thought was not an unpleasant one though Henry felt his stomach twist all the same. He had long had his list of requirements for the lady he was to marry and being a bluestocking was certainly not one of them! And yet, as he turned to continue walking alongside her, Henry recognized that the desire to stay in her company still lingered. It was not as though, after this conversation, he was finished with her and was eager now to step away. Instead, his heart wanted to be with her for just a little longer... and that was something that gave him pause. It had all come about rather unexpectedly and now, as they began to speak of other things, Henry knew he would have to give it a good deal of consideration.

It might change everything.

CHAPTER FOURTEEN

"Might I ask what it is that you are doing?"

Lydia started in surprise, turning quickly to see her mother striding towards her.

"I am reading." There was very little point in attempting to hide this from her, given that there was a pile of books to her left. "That is all."

"Reading?" Her mother seemed to rush towards her all the more quickly, her eyes narrowing. "You are permitted to read novels but nothing like *this*!" She pointed one long finger at the history book which Lydia had sitting to the right hand side of her, turning her sharp eyes towards her and Lydia did her best not to shirk from the angry look in her mother's glare.

"I – I am doing some reading for the Duke."

This deflated her mother in an instant. Slowly, her shoulders lowered, her hand fell back to her side and the angry look faded from her eyes.

"The Duke?"

Lydia nodded, relieved that she was able to tell the truth. "Yes, Mama. The Duke has shown an interest in a particular subject and when I told him I was a little knowledgeable about the area in question, we spoke at length on it."

"Oh." Lady Hampshire tilted her head. "I did notice – though I have not said anything as yet – that he appeared to be quite taken with you on your walk yesterday afternoon."

Forcing a smile, Lydia tried to think quickly about what might suit her mother to know of, for she certainly could not tell her the truth. "He said that he knew the history of his estate and I told him what I knew of it. That is all."

"Then it appears to have done you some good, this *learning* that you do." Her mother sniffed superiorly. "Though it is just as well that he has not thought of it as displeasing as so many other gentlemen might have done!"

"Then... you do not mind if I read a little more? I think that he and I are to have another conversation soon and I think he would be delighted to know that I have spent more time studying the subject."

Her mother considered this, then nodded, just as Lydia had suspected she would. "I suppose, if it is under those circumstances, then I can permit it."

"Thank you, Mama."

Lydia turned her attention back to her books, ignoring her mother as best she could and praying that she would soon take her leave. Much to her relief, she did precisely that and Lydia was able to continue with her studying.

Thus far, she had learned that Lord Chesterfield had been an excellent steward of his wealth. He was a well-respected fellow and had even managed to further his estate by purchasing some more land, though that had come a few years before the loss of the heirlooms. Lydia was not certain that it connected him to the theft, and thus, she had turned her attention to the next gentleman. Lord Montrose was also a gentleman of excellent means, though his estate had been a little more difficult to study given that it was in Scotland. She had considered his son, Lord Gellatly, but again, there had been difficulty in finding what she could out about him. It was still a possibility that *he* was the thief, she considered, though the Duke himself might have to do a little more in terms of discovering what he could about the fellow.

Thus, the only gentleman that was left for her to study was Lord Dunford. Her family was already well acquainted with his, given that he had invited them to his soiree of late on since he was already acquainted with her father. That did not mean that Lydia had any knowledge of who he was or what sort of character he had. Nor did she know much about his estate nor his standing and, with that in her head, she set to her task with relish. It delighted her to learn and to study and this, given that there was an even weightier cause behind it, made it all the more of a pleasure.

～

"You have found out some more, I think?"

Lydia glanced up at her friend, then rose from where she had been sitting, finding her back a little stiff. "Thank you for coming with me to the library again, Sophie. I confess that I was a little frustrated that I could not find what I needed to about Lord Dunford."

"But you have now?"

Lydia nodded slowly, though she drew her brows together as she spoke. "I have found something, yes, but it is not all that I wanted to discover. Lord Dunford's estate is in good standing, his tenants are happy and contented and his family are all held in high esteem in society."

"But?" Sophie tilted her head. "I can see from your expression that there is something that troubles you."

Lydia smiled briefly. "There *is* something that has caught my interest, I shall agree with you on that."

"And what is that?"

Taking a deep breath and considering carefully what she was to say, Lydia gestured to the papers she had been reading. "It is to say that there were some repairs made to the manor house in the year that the heirlooms were taken. However, they had been noted and were expected to take place some five years before then. It is noted simply in the history of the house and the writer has not stated as to why such repairs were delayed."

"That is interesting, certainly." Sophie's eyes rounded. "It could be, then, that *he* is – "

"I must keep that to my thoughts only," Lydia interrupted, keeping her voice low for fear that someone else would hear them. She had told Sophie all that had taken place between herself and the Duke, knowing she would receive her friend's support. "Next, I must tell Melrose what I have discovered and he – "

"Melrose?" Sophie's eyes rounded, the edge of her mouth quirking upwards. "Did you just speak of the Duke in such an *intimate* manner?"

Lydia flushed, heat pouring into her. "He suggested that I do so, given that he did not refer to me as *Lady* Lydia but only Lydia." She tried to push away her friend's gasp of astonishment, trying to pretend that she had not felt anything in that moment. "It means nothing, I am sure."

"I am not so sure!" Sophie leaned closer, her voice a whisper now. "My dear, what if the Duke of Melrose has an interest in you that goes beyond what you are able to offer him as regards your assistance?"

Lydia shook her head. "My dear friend, you cannot think – "

"And look how red your cheeks are when I suggest it!" Sophie's eyes widened and she grasped Lydia's hand. "You must be truthful with me, Lydia. Are you drawn to the Duke?"

Lydia did not know how to answer. If she was to be honest with Sophie, then she would have to admit that yes, there was something in her that was drawn to the Duke, something that she desired about him which seemed to continually pull her closer. Their conversation in the park, the waltz he had pulled her into – both of those things had confirmed to her that her interest in the Duke was not solely in the lost heirlooms.

"Lydia!" Sophie exclaimed, only to clap one hand over her mouth as she ducked her head, clearly aware that she had spoken much too loudly.

"Please, Sophie." Lydia closed her eyes and let out a small sigh, shaking her head as she did so. "You cannot push me to tell you something that I am entirely uncertain of myself."

"Then you *are* interested in a closer connection with him?"

Lydia swallowed tightly, looking away from her friend. To admit this aloud would be very difficult indeed, for what would happen if he did not feel anything in exchange? He was a very handsome and amiable gentleman who spoke well and whose conversation drew her in, and his kindness towards her had been pleasing indeed. In addition, had he not also apologized for his lack of consideration when it came to bluestockings? Had he not told her that he was sorry for his previous harshness? That was a gentleman indeed who said such a thing as that!

"I dare not even *think* about what it is that my heart says," she answered, a little hoarsely. "Sophie, I am afraid." Opening her eyes, she looked straight into Sophie's face and saw her friend's expression soften.

"Oh, my dear." Sophie squeezed Lydia's hand gently. "There is nothing to be afraid of! To have feelings for a particular gentleman is not in the least bit worrisome!"

"No?"

"Of course it is not!" Sophie leaned a little closer. "You have nothing to be afraid of."

Lydia's throat squeezed as she fought back a rush of tears. "But what if he does not feel anything for me? What am I to do then?"

Sophie smiled. "I am sure that there is no need for you to worry. And if it should come to it, then... " Her smile faded. "Then that will be difficult but you do not need to shirk back from that now. It is good that you are willing to admit to what you feel, my dear, though I must confess myself a little surprised!"

"Because I thought so poorly of him and made my feelings on that subject known?"

With a grin, Sophie nodded. "Precisely."

"Things have changed for me since he first shared with me about the heirlooms," Lydia answered, truthfully. "He has been very honest with me, stating that his opinions on bluestockings are no longer the ones he holds to himself. In that regard, I have found him quite altered from my first impression!"

Sophie smiled. "I can see that. Then all I would say is, continue with what you are doing *and* with what you feel, and, in time, consider sharing it all with him."

Hearing this, Lydia flinched but said nothing, aware that her desire to keep her feelings entirely to herself was not a reasonable one. Yes, she *would* have to speak to the Duke about her heart for, if her feelings continued to grow, then she would have no place for them within her and they would bubble up until she had nothing but pain and anguish from trying to push them down.

"I will think about doing so," she said to Sophie, though her friend chuckled lightly at this, as though Lydia was being foolish. "Thank you for your understanding and your advice."

Sophie smiled. "Always."

CHAPTER FIFTEEN

Henry paid not even the smallest bit of attention to any of the ladies who were, he knew, trying to capture his attention. Lord Kinlaw's ball was in full swing and yet there was only one person he was looking for.

And strangely, it was not because of the heirlooms or any wondering as to what she had discovered. Instead, it was because he wanted to see her and be in her company.

Henry rubbed one hand over his chin, considering. Thus far, he had been aware of his growing affection for Lady Lydia but ever since they had danced the waltz together, ever since he had realized just how much of a marvel she was, they had grown with a fierceness that now took his breath away whenever he even though about it.

"She is just over there."

A familiar voice caught Henry's attention and he turned to see Lord Kendall pointing to the left of the ballroom.

"With her mother."

Henry nodded, choosing not to say anything but all too

aware that his friend knew of his interest in the lady. "I thank you."

"Have you made progress?"

With a smile, Henry nodded. "Not I but Lady Lydia. Indeed, my friend, I have found her so utterly remarkable that I realize now how foolish I was to ever state that bluestockings were worthy of being shunned by society!" His smile faded as the heat of embarrassment rose in his face instead. "She has done more for me than I ever imagined and even if I were not to find the truth about the heirlooms, I should find myself contented all the same."

Lord Kendall's eyebrows lifted. "Truly?"

Henry nodded. "Truly. The more I consider her, the more I see just how incredible a young lady she is – and how foolish I was to ever turn my head away from her."

"Then I wish you well," came the reply, as Lord Kendall slapped Henry on the shoulder. "Do excuse me. I must go and take my dance – my *first* dance of the evening, for I have taken two – with Lady Miriam."

With a chuckle, Henry watched as his friend stepped away before he too went in search of the particular young lady *he* desired to see. His heart quickened as he caught sight of her red curls dancing as she moved across the floor, safe in the arms of another gentleman.

That displeased him a great deal though Henry did not let the feeling settle. There was nothing wrong with Lady Lydia dancing, he reminded himself. It was what every eligible young lady ought to be doing... though could he help it if he desired to be the only one with her in his arms?

Goodness, these feelings have taken a swift hold of my heart! With a wry smile on his face, Henry contented himself with watching the remainder of the cotillion, determining to draw close to Lady Lydia the moment the dance finished.

He saw the very moment that she became aware of him watching her. Her eyes rounded just a little only for her to smile back at him, her green eyes warming and a gentle flush coming into her cheeks. Henry's heart leaped up furiously, his own lips curving into a smile as the urge to rush forward and speak with her grew ever stronger.

Instead, he lingered where he was, watching as she bade the gentleman farewell and then, after a moment, came directly towards him. The closer she came, the more furiously his heart beat, the more desperate he became for her to be near to him. Waiting patiently still, he could not help the sigh of relief when she finally came to join him, inclining her head as she smiled.

"Your Grace. Good evening."

"Good evening," he said, taking her hand and bowing over it, resisting the urge to brush his lips over her skin. "I am delighted to see you this evening."

"I am sure you are," she answered, "for you must have been most impatient to hear what I have learned."

Henry shook his head, a slight frown on his forehead. "No, that is not what I meant." He watched surprise come into her face. "I mean only that I am very glad to see *you*, Lydia. It does not matter a great deal what it is you have or have not discovered, I shall have delight in your company regardless."

This made her cheeks warm all the more and she looked away, perhaps uncertain as to what she ought to say.

"Should you like to dance this evening?" he asked, as she quickly glanced back towards him. "I must hope that you have some dances remaining!"

"I do, yes. Thank you." She handed him her dance card

and waited, though Henry found it a struggle to take his gaze away from hers. He was seeing her in a new way now, recognizing just how much he had in her and desiring now to claim her for his own. Watching her dance with another gentleman had brought about feelings of envy and jealousy though that had surprised him a little. What was it that he wanted from her? What was it that he wanted for himself? After the matter of the heirlooms was at an end, would he be contented to step away from her for good? Or did he want something more?

I want something more.

"Here." He wrote his name down not only for the waltz but also for the polka, swallowing tightly as he did so before handing it back to her. Watching her response, he could not help but smile at the swift intake of breath he heard coming from her, seeing how her eyes widened all the more as she looked back at him. "If that is quite all right with you, Lydia?" he asked, gently. "I know what questions this might bring but I am not afraid of them."

She blinked rapidly, her eyes seeming to glisten for just a moment though she quickly smiled and shook her head. "No, neither am I," she answered, a softness about her voice that betrayed her deep emotion. "Thank you, Melrose. You are most considerate."

He wanted to say more, wanted to tell her that his feelings and affections had exploded of late but instead, he merely smiled back at her and said nothing.

"You will want to know what I have learned, of course," she said, changing their conversation in a moment and setting all feelings and emotions aside. "I have learned a great deal, for I have been permitted to study and read just as much as I have desired!"

"And how has that been possible?"

She giggled, a light, airy sound that made him grin. "I informed my mother that it was for you that I was doing such a thing, that you were delighted in our prior conversations and suddenly, all was quite well."

Grinning, Henry offered her his arm. "Then she will not mind if we take a turn about the room, I hope? I can see her nearby and, no doubt, she will follow."

Lady Lydia took his arm without hesitating. "She will be glad, I am sure." They began to walk and it was as if the rest of the ballroom faded to nothing. All he cared about was Lady Lydia's company, all he wanted and desired was to be beside her. With a contented sigh, he looked down at her and smiled, seeing the same happiness he felt reflected in her eyes.

"I do not think that it can be your uncle."

Henry's eyebrows lifted. "No?"

She shook her head. "No. He is a gentleman in good standing and what I have learned about his estate and the area he resides in is that there has been nothing of note as regards his finances. Indeed, he furthered his estate by purchasing land, though that came before the loss of your father's heirlooms."

"I see. Though," Henry continued, "he does have a scar."

Lady Lydia nodded. "He does, yes."

"Then Lord Montrose?"

A slight wince crossed Lady Lydia's expression. "I cannot say for certain. I have found it a little more difficult to find information as regards his estate and the like, given that it is in Scotland."

Henry nodded, his brow furrowing. "He was well acquainted with my father and would have known about the heirlooms, I am sure. Yes, he resides in Scotland but I am sure that he came to London on occasion."

"All the same," Lady Lydia continued, gently, "it may have nothing to do with him."

Hearing the hesitation in her voice, Henry turned to look at her, coming to a short pause in their walk around the ballroom. "Then you believe that Lord Dunford is the most likely culprit?"

Lady Lydia pressed her lips tight together. "I – I cannot say for certain," she said, slowly, "for it would not be my place to suggest such a thing. However, what I learned in my study was that there were a good many repairs that were needed at the estate and he did not manage to do any, not for a long time."

A jolt ran through Henry, realizing what she was saying before she had even said it. "And yet, he managed to complete his repairs only after my heirlooms were taken."

Lady Lydia nodded slowly, her eyes searching his face.

"Though he has no scar on his face," Henry continued, muttering now to himself, "though he does have that large beard which means that his face is, in many ways, hidden."

"Did he always have it?"

Scrunching up his nose, Henry thought for a few moments and then shrugged. "I could not say."

"Then what will you do?"

The polka was announced before Henry could say anything and taking a breath, he looked towards her. "I shall dance the polka with you and then enjoy the rest of the evening," he declared, determinedly. "And once that is over, I shall permit myself to consider all that must be done." Smiling, he turned and inclined his head, offering her his hand rather than his arm. "Shall we step out to dance together, Lydia?"

With a look of surprise etching into her expression, swiftly followed by a delighted smile, she accepted his hand. "Thank you, Your Grace. I should be very glad to do so indeed."

"Lord Montrose, good evening." Henry inclined his head, aware that time was short. The ball was now at an end and every gentleman and lady were making their way to their carriages, Given the crush, it was taking a very long time indeed for some of them to get to their carriage.

"Good evening, Your Grace." Lord Montrose nodded, a weariness in his expression. "I hope you have enjoyed the ball? I did see you dancing twice this evening with the same young lady!"

Henry chuckled, refusing to let the remark take a hold. He had done such a thing deliberately and had known that the *ton* would take notice. That was not the reason for his conversation with this gentleman. "Indeed. I am, as you know, as yet unwed and I must consider taking a bride! You will understand, I am sure."

Lord Montrose nodded. "Indeed."

"Your son will have the same requirement," Henry continued, with a smile as Lord Montrose chuckled. "I do hope he has success!"

"If he put a little more time into courting and a little less into cards, then I am sure he would do very well indeed!" came the laughing response. "Ah, here is another carriage."

Henry nodded. "Yes, that is mine. My driver, Stanley, is an excellent sort." As he spoke, he kept a keen eye upon Lord Montrose but the gentleman did not give any sort of reaction. There was no flinching, no sudden strain in his expression, and certainly no tension in his voice as he bid him good evening.

"It was very pleasant to speak with you again, Your Grace." Lord Montrose smiled. "Good evening."

"Good evening." Henry nodded to himself as he made his way towards the carriage, feeling quite certain now that Lord Montrose had not taken the heirlooms. It had been the only area of uncertainty for him, though, to his knowledge, Lord Montrose bore no scar upon his face. The mention of his father's driver – Stanley – had been a test to see whether or not Lord Montrose would show any sort of reaction but there had been none.

That left either his uncle, Lord Chesterfield, who, given what Lady Lydia had discovered, had purchased additional land *before* the heirlooms had been taken. That did not mean that he was not the one who had taken them though Henry could not think as to why he would have done so. Thus, the only person he was left to consider – aside from Lord Northstone, given that he was no longer with them – was Lord Dunford.

Henry climbed into his carriage, a sense of satisfaction growing in his heart.

Though what shall you do if you do not find the truth? What if Lord Dunford denies it? What if nothing occurs to show you where the heirlooms now reside?

A frown climbed into his expression as he considered, turning his head to look out at the dark streets as the carriage made its way through London. Would he continue on his pursuit to find out the truth? Or could it be that, with all that he now had in Lady Lydia, that he might, instead, realize where the true treasure lay?

CHAPTER SIXTEEN

Lydia smiled as she watched Sophie and her husband walk, arm in arm, a little ahead of her. St James' Park was rather busy but given that it was such a fine day, Lydia was not in the least bit surprised. Many of the *ton* would want to be seen by other members of society as well as noting who else was present and thus, a growing crowd was assembling across the grass and blocking the paths on occasion! Hearing Sophie laugh at something her husband had said made Lydia's smile grow all the more, glad that her friend had found such a delightful gentleman to be her husband. Someone who, she knew, cherished Sophie and encouraged her love of learning.

If only it could be the same for me.

The hint of envy in her heart made Lydia's smile crack and she tried to push it away just as quickly as she could, a little surprised when the Duke of Melrose entered into her thoughts. At the very start of the Season, he had been the very last person that she had ever considered would be supportive of a bluestocking! And yet, in their acquaintance, in their ever improving connection, he had changed so significantly, that she knew he would champion her, should she ask him to do so! The words he spoke to her, the gratitude, the humbleness of him had all shown her just how much he had changed in his attitude and opinions. No longer would she call him arrogant, no longer would she consider him selfish or disagreeable. Instead, he meant so much to her that her heart was practically filled with him.

"We are neglecting you, I think."

Lydia looked up as Sophie turned to her. "Here I am, having invited you to join us, leaving you to walk alone!"

"It is quite all right." Lydia smiled at her friend. "I am quite contented, I assure you. My thoughts are many and I am more than happy to walk quietly."

"You think on him, then?" Sophie chuckled as Lydia flushed and looked away. "I shall not tease you, my dear. Especially when I see him approaching with what, I think, is a purposeful step!"

Her head lifted instantly, her eyes searching the grounds, only to fasten upon the Duke of Melrose coming directly towards her. He was already smiling and Lydia could not help but return it, her heart quickening as he bowed, thrilled to see him again – even though it had been less than a day since they had last been in company together!

"Your Grace, I think you shall soon have all the *ton* speaking of yourself and my *dear* friend, should you continue to shower such attention upon her!"

Lydia shot Sophie a sharp look, aware of the heat that began to curl through her as her friend continued on, ignoring the look that Lydia had given her.

"First, you danced your very first waltz of the Season with her, only to then dance twice with her last evening which is something you have not done as yet either! I do hope you are aware that society is already beginning to whisper."

The Duke chuckled and nodded. "Yes, Lady Markham, I am well aware of it. Though I do not care one jot as to what society will say and I have, be assured, made certain that Lady Lydia is quite contented also. I would not bring her any embarrassment, I assure you."

Sophie nodded and smiled, though she winked at Lydia in a less than surreptitious manner, making Lydia's face burn all the more. "That is good to hear, Your Grace. You understand that I speak only out of concern, I hope?"

"I do." The Duke finally turned his attention back to Lydia, his face a little flushed. "Might you be willing to walk with me for a time, Lady Lydia?"

"I should be glad to." Relieved to step away from Sophie for fear that she would say something more, Lydia took the Duke's arm and set off along the path, certain that Sophie and her husband would stay near. "I – I am sorry if anything Lady Markham said brought you any embarrassment. I am sure she did not mean it."

Thankfully, the Duke chuckled. "Not in the least. She is concerned for you and I can understand that." He glanced at her, then frowned. "Though I do hope that you are not concerned about all that society will say. I am not, though that is because I do not care what they think. My own intentions are all that I think of."

Lydia pressed her lips together but did not say anything, wondering what it was that the Duke meant by his intentions. What intentions did he have towards her? She could only pray that they were not that their friendship would end once the truth about the heirlooms were discovered.

"I did enjoy your latest article in The London Chronicle," he told her, smiling down into her eyes. "You have a great talent, Lydia."

Her heart leaped at his compliment and at the way his hazel eyes swirled. "I thank you."

"I think that I – "

"Oh, what a fine afternoon it is!"

An unfamiliar voice broke through their conversation and Lydia was forced to pull her attention away from the Duke, seeing another fellow coming towards them. It was not Lord Kendall, but an older gentleman with a greying beard and a rather jolly face. It took her a few moments to remember, only to recall that this was none other than Lord Dunford.

Her hand tightened on the Duke's arm and he threw her a quick look, understanding in his eyes.

"Good afternoon, Lord Dunford," he began, as Lydia bobbed a quick curtsy. "Yes, it is indeed. I am out walking with Lady Lydia, as you can see."

"Of course, of course!" Lord Dunford beamed at Lydia as though her presence was enough to delight him. "How wonderful to see you out here again, Melrose. You appear to be in better spirits than you were at my soiree!" He laughed at this but Lydia bit her lip, a little concerned over what the Duke might say to this.

Thankfully, she did not have to worry.

"Indeed, I was in low spirits," the Duke agreed, shaking his head. "But that is because I had only just learned that the story in The London Chronicle was, in fact, quite true."

This made Lord Dunford's face freeze into a fixed expression, and Lydia's eyebrows lifted as she watched him.

"I am sure you know the one I mean," the Duke continued, letting out a long sigh. "Do you not?"

Lord Dunford's smile was no longer as bright as before.

"If you are speaking of the heirlooms, then yes. That was a strange story indeed, was it not?"

The Duke tipped his head just a little. "I am not certain I would consider it *strange*, no. You see, my father had not told me anything about the heirlooms and had also, for whatever reason, instructed my mother to say nothing on the subject either. Though I now realize why that was, of course."

Lydia said nothing, holding her breath as she waited for Lord Dunford to respond. Would he respond to the Duke's remark or merely shrug off the comment before turning the conversation to other things?

"Might I ask why that is?" Lord Dunford's voice had, to Lydia's mind, become a little strained. "I knew your father well, as you know. I am surprised that he kept the theft of the heirlooms from you."

"Indeed but it was because he did not know who it was." The Duke sniffed and then lifted his chin. "However, since the writing of that article, I have heard from my mother. She told me of those that my father suspected of stealing the heirlooms."

A slight pallor came into Lord Dunford's face.

"And even more so, I found the driver, Stanley," the Duke continued, making Lydia's eyes flare though she did not look up at him, wondering if this was the truth or if there was something of a pretense here. "And he has told me all."

Lord Dunford blinked furiously, going a furious red before turning very pale indeed. Lydia blinked quickly, her breath hitching in her chest as she realized, in one swift, wonderful moment, that the truth had been discovered. There was no doubt in her mind now that Lord Dunford *had* been the one to steal the heirlooms.

"You grew your beard to cover the scar," she breathed, her eyes fixing to Lord Dunford as the Duke nodded in evident agreement. "The late Duke injured you, did he not? And this was the only way you could hide it."

Lord Dunford shook his head furiously. "No, that is *preposterous*."

"You may as well be honest, Dunford." The Duke's voice had taken on a commanding tone. "It is just as well for you that we are speaking out here in public, rather than standing in your drawing room or study, which was where I had intended to confront you."

This sent a quake through Lord Dunford, for he trembled visibly and seemed to shrink before them both. The authority that the Duke presented merely by his stance and firm voice was enough to make Lydia tense, hardly able to imagine what it must feel like for Lord Dunford at this moment! She gripped the Duke's arm all the more tightly, half hoping, half praying that the confession would come and that the Duke would hear all that he needed.

"The truth, Dunford." Again, the Duke spoke but this time, his voice was lower and yet held even greater weight than before. "I will hear it from you now."

Lord Dunford dropped his head and heaved out a great long breath, still shaking. The Duke stood firm and Lydia stayed precisely where she was also, feeling as if the very air around them held its breath as it waited.

Then, he spoke.

"I had no other choice." The heaviness in Lord Dunford's frame was reflected in his voice and as he lifted his head, he looked straight into the Duke's eyes, desperation there. "My estate was falling to the ground. My late father had done nothing to prepare me for just how much debt was to fall upon me! I had married before he passed from this life and it was only then, once I took ownership of the estate, that I realized just how much difficulty I was in."

The Duke scowled. "Thus, you used your friendship with my father to steal the heirlooms from him. And you did so for your own purposes."

"I would not have killed him!" Lord Dunford exclaimed, as though this somehow made the situation a good deal better. "I wanted the heirlooms. I knew that he was to go to London to fetch them, for he had informed me of it."

"And the driver?"

Lord Dunford closed his eyes. "He was easy enough to bribe."

Lydia let out a slow breath, feeling every part of her body tingling. The truth had been revealed though it did not return the heirlooms to the Duke. She presumed that Lord Dunford had used them for his own requirements.

"You took the diamonds from my father," the Duke said, speaking slowly as though every word was a weight. "You pretended to be a highwayman, bribed his driver, and then threatened him with death. And all because you needed money."

Lord Dunford dropped his head again, an anguished exclamation breaking from his lips. "I was in a state of despair! I could not be declared impoverished, for what would that do to my family? To my reputation? I had to find a way out of the difficulty I had been placed in."

"The Duke suspected you," Lydia said, quietly, as Lord Dunford continued to keep his gaze low. "No doubt he realized that you had managed to make the improvements required to your estate only a short while after the heirlooms were taken."

"You used the diamonds to pay for it all." With a hiss of

breath, the Duke shook his head. "And still, you pretended to be my father's friend."

There came no response from Lord Dunford and Lydia glanced up at the Duke, wondering what it was he would do now.

"I will consider what must be done," the Duke said, after a long moment. "Excuse us, Lord Dunford. I have no desire to linger in your presence."

Much to Lydia's surprise, the Duke led her away from the broken gentleman, his steps quick and hasty. Lydia walked alongside him without question, saying nothing and barely daring a glance up towards him given the stony expression on his face. They walked for some time in silence, with the Duke not even acknowledging any of the greetings from others who walked along the park paths. Her heart was beating rather quickly, her stomach twisting as she prayed that the Duke would, somehow, find a way to recover.

"Goodness."

It was the first word he had said in some time and, his steps slowing, the Duke reached across with his free hand and set it on hers. He let out another long sigh and Lydia finally found herself able to hold his gaze, surprised to see the heavy expression fading away.

"I cannot quite believe that the truth has been discovered! I was not certain that he would confess to it all."

"But if you spoke to the driver, then –"

"Alas, I did not." He winced. "I confess that I told a mistruth, though that is only because I felt it right to do so."

She nodded slowly, understanding. "You have your confession, that is all that is important. You know what happened to them and who took them."

"And why," he added, shaking his head before rubbing

one hand over his eyes. "Now that I know the truth, I confess that I do not quite know what to do."

Lydia said nothing, not certain that she could offer any advice in such a situation.

"I shall think on it," he said, after a short while. "Thank you for all you have done for me, Lydia."

"But of course." She smiled and made to continue walking, only for a frown to appear in the Duke's expression. "Is there something wrong?"

He frowned all the harder, only to smile, as though the sunshine had suddenly broken through a great and heavy cloud to shine brightness on them all. "I feel a good deal lighter," he said, making her smile. "And that is *all* because of you."

EPILOGUE

"I know what it is that I want to do."

Henry strode through the door of Lord and Lady Hampshire's drawing room, heedless to who else was present in the room.

"Your... Your Grace!" Lady Lydia practically leaped to her feet, though Lady Markham –there to take tea with her friend – smiled and rose to her feet before walking quietly out of the room.

"I know what I want to do, Lydia," Henry told her, filled with that strange and sudden determination that had flooded him from the very moment he had awoken this morning. "I have decided." Coming closer to her, he took both of her hands in his, his heart thumping wildly.

"About the heirlooms?" Lady Lydia blinked, her eyes round as she gazed up at him. "Or Lord Dunford?"

A smile touched the edge of his mouth. "I have decided on that, yes, though that is not what I am speaking of at present," he told her, trying to speak a little more gently now. "I have realized something. I awoke this morning without that burden upon my shoulders, without the wonderings about the heirlooms sitting in my mind and that has brought me such clarity, it is as though I am seeing everything in a new light!"

She blinked again but said nothing, her lips in a small circle of surprise.

"The heirlooms were important to me," Henry continued, quickly, "but now that I know what happened to them and where they have gone, I do not have to worry about that any longer. There is nothing I can do to recover them and nothing I can bring upon Lord Dunford by way of consequence." Lifting one shoulder lightly, he pressed her hands. "It is not right what he did, of course, but there is no recourse. A letter came from him this morning and I have his apology – his profuse apology – and his promise to make some sort of reparation but I have come to see that such a thing is not of great value or importance to me. Having the diamonds returned would have brought me contentment, yes, but it would not have brought me joy." Leaning down just a little, he looked keenly into her eyes. "You do."

Watching her expression carefully, Henry waited for her response. When he had woken this morning, he had realized, in a single moment, that the only thing he cared about now was whether or not Lady Lydia might continue in their acquaintance... and just how much he wanted her to be by his side. His heart, now free of the questions and concerns over the heirlooms, had laid out his emotions quite plainly, showing him just how much of an affection and desire he had for Lady Lydia.

He could only pray that she felt something similar.

"I do not quite know what to say, Melrose." Her voice was quiet, her words halting. "This is all so extraordinary that I am quite overwhelmed."

Henry pressed his lips together, his spirits sinking just a

little. "I do not mean to overpower you. It is my determination that makes me speak so."

"Determination?" She looked up at him now, questions in her eyes. "What does your determination want?"

This question made Henry smile, the answer already on his lips. "I want to court you, Lydia. I want to consider engagement and matrimony for, through all of this, I have come to see that though the jewels were valuable, what I have in you is all the more precious. You are extraordinary! You have made me reconsider my own views, have made me see my own arrogance and, despite that, I have been given nothing but compassion, understanding, and more! You have, willingly, given me your time and your energy, showing me that you have more ability and knowledge than I had ever thought to credit you with. I have learned so much from being in your company, Lydia, and I do not want our connection now to come to an end."

She nodded slowly, though there was no smile on her lips. "Thank you for saying such things."

"You... you do not appear to be happy." Henry frowned now, his hands gentling on hers. "Is there something wrong?"

Closing her eyes, Lady Lydia blew out a breath before nodding to herself, as if finding the courage to speak. "Yes, there is. Though I value your words and appreciate your compliments, I confess that my heart holds more for you than just that." Opening her eyes, she looked back at him, a gentle glistening of tears there. "I think I have come to care for you, Melrose. The beginnings of love are playing about my heart and though I do not require you to have the same within your heart, I want you to know what it is that I feel."

Astonishment hit Henry right between the eyes, making

him take a step back. She cared for him? He could hardly dare to believe it! Shaking his head, he let out a quiet laugh. He saw her frown and, upon seeing that, pulled her quickly into his arms.

She gasped.

"My dear Lydia, you must forgive me for my foolishness." Whispering now, he lifted one hand and brushed it lightly down her cheek. "When I came to London, I had a list of requirements that any lady of my consideration must meet before I would even *think* about courtship. But then, I met you." His thumb touched the edges of her lips and desire kicked in him, hard. "I did not think that I would ever fall in love with a bluestocking, but now I confess to you that I have done so. I did not use the right words, did not express to you the depths of my heart for you but I swear to you, Lydia, that all you feel for me is just as I feel for you."

She softened in his arms, her eyes searching his face as if desperate to find the truth.

"I spoke of how much I value you, how much I admire you but I did not tell you how much I have come to care for you," he finished, lowering his head just a little. "You speak of the beginnings of love and that is precisely what I feel. I want to court you, want to engage myself to you and, in the end, marry you for I do not think that I could be a day without you, Lydia. You are my diamond, you are my treasure. You are all that matters to me."

A gentle sigh broke from her lips as she lifted one hand and settled it against his heart, the other going around his neck. "Then it seems that we are both in agreement, Melrose," she murmured, as his head began to lower. "Though can you abide courting and marrying a bluestocking?"

A quiet chuckle broke from his lips as he clasped her to him all the more tightly. "I look forward to it," he whispered, before gently bringing his lips to hers.

MY DEAR READER

Thank you for reading and supporting my books! I hope this story brought you some escape from the real world into the always captivating Regency world. A good story, especially one with a happy ending, just brightens your day and makes you feel good! If you enjoyed the book, would you leave a review on Amazon? Reviews are always appreciated.

Below is a complete list of all my books! Why not click and see if one of them can keep you entertained for a few hours?

The Duke's Daughters Series
The Duke's Daughters: A Sweet Regency Romance Boxset
A Rogue for a Lady
My Restless Earl
Rescued by an Earl
In the Arms of an Earl
The Reluctant Marquess (Prequel)

A Smithfield Market Regency Romance
The Smithfield Market Romances: A Sweet Regency Romance Boxset
The Rogue's Flower
Saved by the Scoundrel
Mending the Duke
The Baron's Malady

The Returned Lords of Grosvenor Square
The Returned Lords of Grosvenor Square: A Regency Romance Boxset
The Waiting Bride
The Long Return
The Duke's Saving Grace
A New Home for the Duke

The Spinsters Guild
The Spinsters Guild: A Sweet Regency Romance Boxset
A New Beginning
The Disgraced Bride
A Gentleman's Revenge
A Foolish Wager
A Lord Undone

Convenient Arrangements
Convenient Arrangements: A Regency Romance Collection
A Broken Betrothal
In Search of Love
Wed in Disgrace
Betrayal and Lies
A Past to Forget
Engaged to a Friend

Landon House
Landon House: A Regency Romance Boxset
Mistaken for a Rake
A Selfish Heart
A Love Unbroken
A Christmas Match
A Most Suitable Bride

An Expectation of Love

Second Chance Regency Romance
Second Chance Regency Romance Boxset
Loving the Scarred Soldier
Second Chance for Love
A Family of her Own
A Spinster No More

Soldiers and Sweethearts
Soldiers and Sweethearts Boxset
To Trust a Viscount
Whispers of the Heart
Dare to Love a Marquess
Healing the Earl
A Lady's Brave Heart

Ladies on their Own: Governesses and Companions
Ladies on their Own Boxset
More Than a Companion
The Hidden Governess
The Companion and the Earl
More than a Governess
Protected by the Companion

Lost Fortunes, Found Love
Lost Fortunes, Found Love Boxset
A Viscount's Stolen Fortune
For Richer, For Poorer
Her Heart's Choice
A Dreadful Secret
Their Forgotten Love
His Convenient Match

Only for Love

Only for Love : A Clean Regency Boxset
The Heart of a Gentleman
A Lord or a Liar
The Earl's Unspoken Love
The Viscount's Unlikely Ally
The Highwayman's Hidden Heart
Miss Millington's Unexpected Suitor

Waltzing with Wallflowers

The Wallflower's Unseen Charm
The Wallflower's Midnight Waltz
Wallflower Whispers
The Ungainly Wallflower
The Determined Wallflower
The Wallflower's Secret (Revenge of the Wallflowers series)
The Wallflower's Choice

Whispers of the Ton

The Truth about the Earl
The Truth about the Rogue
The Truth about the Marquess
The Truth about the Viscount
The Truth about the Duke

Christmas in London Series
The Uncatchable Earl
The Undesirable Duke

Christmas Kisses Series
Christmas Kisses Box Set
The Lady's Christmas Kiss
The Viscount's Christmas Queen

Her Christmas Duke

Christmas Stories
Love and Christmas Wishes: Three Regency Romance Novellas
A Family for Christmas
Mistletoe Magic: A Regency Romance
Heart, Homes & Holidays: A Sweet Romance Anthology

Happy Reading!
All my love,
Rose

A SNEAK PEEK OF THE TRUTH ABOUT THE EARL

PROLOGUE

"I was very sorry to hear of the death of your husband."

Lady Norah Essington gave the older lady a small smile, which she did not truly feel. "I thank you. You are very kind." Her tone was dull but Norah had no particular concerns as regarded either how she sounded or how she appeared to the lady. She was, yet again, alone in the world, and as things stood, was uncertain as to what her future would be.

"You did not care for him, I think."

Norah's gaze returned to Lady Gillingham's with such force, the lady blinked in surprise and leaned back a fraction in her chair.

"I mean no harm by such words, I assure you. I –"

"You have made an assumption, Lady Gillingham, and I would be glad if you should keep such notions to yourself." Norah lifted her chin but heard her voice wobble. "I should prefer to mourn the loss of my husband without whispers or gossip chasing around after me."

Lady Gillingham smiled, reached forward, and settled one hand over Norah's. "But of course."

Norah turned her head, trying to silently signal that the meeting was now at an end. She was not particularly well acquainted with the lady and, as such, would be glad of her departure so that she might sit alone and in peace. Besides which, if Lady Gillingham had been as bold as to make such a claim as that directly to Norah herself, then what would she think to say to the *ton*? Society might be suddenly full of whispers about Norah and her late husband—and then what would she do?

"I have upset you. Forgive me."

Norah dared a glance at Lady Gillingham, taking in the gentle way her eyes searched Norah's face and the small, soft smile on her lips. "I do not wish you to disparage my late husband, Lady Gillingham. Nor do I want to hear such rumors being spread in London – whenever it would be that I would have cause to return."

"I quite understand, and I can assure you I do not have any intention of speaking of any such thing to anyone in society."

"Then why state such a thing in my presence? My husband is only a sennight gone and, as I am sure you are aware, I am making plans to remove myself to his estate."

"Provided you are still welcome there."

Norah closed her eyes, a familiar pain flashing through her heart. "Indeed." Suddenly, she wanted very much for Lady Gillingham to take her leave. This was not at all what she had thought would occur. The lady, she had assumed, would simply express her sympathies and take her leave.

"Again, I have injured you." Lady Gillingham let out a long sigh and then shook her head. "Lady Essington, forgive me. I am speaking out of turn and with great thoughtlessness, which I must apologize for. The truth is, I come here out of genuine concern for you, given that I have been in the very same situation."

Norah drew her eyebrows together. She was aware that Lady Gillingham was widowed but did not know when such a thing had taken place.

"I was, at that time, given an opportunity which I grasped at with both hands. It is a paid position but done most discreetly."

Blinking rapidly, Norah tried to understand what Lady Gillingham meant. "I am to be offered employment?" She shook her head. "Lady Gillingham, that is most kind of you but I assure you I will be quite well. My husband often assured me his brother is a kind, warm-hearted gentleman and I have every confidence that he will take care of me." This was said with a confidence Norah did not truly feel but given the strangeness of this first meeting, she was doing so in an attempt to encourage Lady Gillingham to take her leave. Her late husband had, in fact, warned her about his brother on more than one occasion, telling her he was a selfish, arrogant sort who would not care a jot for anyone other than himself.

"I am very glad to hear of it, but should you find yourself in any difficulty, then I would beg of you to consider this. I have written for the paper for some time and find myself a little less able to do so nowadays. The truth is, Lady Essington, I am a little dull when it comes to society and very little takes place that could be of any real interest to anyone, I am sure."

Growing a little frustrated, Norah spread her hands. "I do not understand you, Lady Gillingham. Perhaps this is not -"

"An opportunity to *write*, Lady Essington." Lady

Gillingham leaned forward in her chair, her eyes suddenly dark and yet sparkling at the same time. "To write about society! Do you understand what I mean?"

Norah shook her head but a small twist of interest flickered in her heart. "No, Lady Gillingham. I am afraid I do not."

The lady smiled and her eyes held fast to Norah's. "*The London Chronicle*, as you know, has society pages. I am sure you have read them?"

Norah nodded slowly, recalling the times she and her mother had pored over the society pages in search of news as to which gentlemen might be worth considering when it came to her future. "I have found them very informative."

"Indeed, I am glad to hear so." Lady Gillingham smiled as if she had something to do with the pages themselves. "There is a rather large column within the society pages that mayhap you have avoided if you are averse to gossip and the like."

Norah shifted uncomfortably in her chair. The truth was, she *had* read them many times over and had been a little too eager to know of the gossip and rumors swirling through London society whilst, at the same time, refusing to speak of them to anyone else for fear of spreading further gossip.

"I can see you understand what it is I am speaking about. Well, Lady Essington, you must realize that someone writes such a column, I suppose?" She smiled and Norah nodded slowly. "*I am that person.*"

Shock spread through Norah's heart and ice filled her chest. Not all of the gossip she had read had been pleasant – indeed, some of it had been so very unfavorable that reputations had been quite ruined.

"You are a little surprised but I must inform you I have

set a great deal of trust in you by revealing this truth." Lady Gillingham's smile had quite faded and instead, Norah was left with a tight-lipped older lady looking back at her with steel in her dark eyes.

"I – I understand."

"Good." Lady Gillingham smiled but there was no lightness in her expression. "The reason I speak to you so, Lady Essington, is to offer you the opportunity in the very same way that I was all those years ago."

For some moments, Norah stared at Lady Gillingham with undisguised confusion. She had no notion as to what the lady meant nor what she wanted and, as such, could only shake her head.

Lady Gillingham sighed. "I am tired of writing my column, Lady Essington. As I have said, it is a paid position and all done very discreetly. I wish to return to my little house in the country and enjoy being away in the quiet countryside rather than the hubbub of London. The funds I have received for writing this particular column have been more than enough over the years and I have managed to save a good deal so that I might retire to the country in comfort."

"I see." Still a little confused, Norah twisted her lips to one side for a few moments. "And you wish for *me* to write this for you?"

"For yourself!" Lady Gillingham flung her hands in the air. "They want to continue the column, for it is *very* popular, and as such, they require someone to write it. I thought that, since you find yourself in much the same situation as I was some years ago, you might be willing to think on it."

Blowing out a long, slow breath, Norah found herself nodding out but quickly stopped it from occurring. "I think I should like to consider it a little longer."

"But of course. You have your mourning period, and thereafter, perhaps you might be willing to give me an answer?"

Norah frowned. "But that is a little over a year away."

"Yes, I am well aware it is a long time, Lady Essington. But I shall finish writing for this Season in the hope that you will take over thereafter. It is, as I am sure you have been able to tell, quite secretive and without any danger."

Norah gave her a small smile, finding her heart flooding with a little relief. "Because you are Mrs. Fullerton," she answered, as Lady Gillingham beamed at her. "You write as Mrs. Fullerton, I should say."

"Indeed, I do. I must, for else society would not wish to have me join them in anything, and then where would I be?" A murmur of laughter broke from her lips as she got to her feet, bringing her prolonged visit to an end. "Consider what I have suggested, my dear. I do not know what your circumstances are at present and I am quite certain you will *not* be aware of them until you return to the late Lord Essington's estate but I am quite sure you would do excellently. You may, of course, write to me whenever you wish with any questions or concerns that I could answer for you."

"I very much appreciate your concern *and* your consideration, Lady Gillingham." Rising to her feet, Norah gave the lady a small curtsy, which was returned. "I shall take the year to consider it."

"Do." Reaching out, Lady Gillingham grasped Norah's hands and held them tightly, her eyes fixed on Norah's. "Do not permit yourself to be pushed aside, Lady Essington. Certain characters might soon determine that you do not deserve what is written on Lord Essington's will but be aware that it cannot be contested. Take what is yours and make certain you do all you can for your comfort. No one will take from you what is rightfully yours, I assure you."

Norah's smile slipped and she could only nod as Lady Gillingham squeezed her hands. She was rather fearful of returning to her late husband's estate and being informed of her situation as regarded her husband's death.

"And you must promise me that you will not speak of this to anyone."

"Of course," Norah promised without hesitation. "I shall not tell a soul, Lady Gillingham. Of that, you can be quite certain."

"Good, I am glad." With another warm smile, Lady Gillingham dropped Norah's hands and made her way to the door. "Good afternoon, Miss Essington. I do hope your sorrow passes quickly."

Norah nodded and smiled but did not respond. Did Lady Gillingham know Norah had never had a kind thought for her husband? That their marriage had been solely because of Lord Essington's desire to have a young, pretty wife by his side rather than due to any real or genuine care or consideration for her? Telling herself silently that such a thing did not matter, Norah waited until Lady Gillingham had quit the room before flopping back into her chair and blowing out a long breath.

Most extraordinary. Biting her lip, Norah considered what Lady Gillingham had offered her. Was it something she would consider? Would she become the next writer of the *London Chronicle* society column? It was employment, but not something Norah could simply ignore.

"I might very well require some extra coin," she murmured to herself, sighing heavily as another rap came at the door. Most likely, this would be another visitor coming to express their sympathy and sorrow. Whilst Norah did not begrudge them, she was finding herself rather weary.

I have a year to consider, she reminded herself, calling for the footman to come into the room. *One year. And then I may very well find myself as the new Mrs. Fullerton.*

CHAPTER ONE

One year later.
Taking the hand of her coachman, Norah descended from the carriage and drew in a long breath.

I am back in London.

The strange awareness that she was quite alone – without companion or chaperone – rushed over her, rendering Norah a little uncomfortable. Wriggling her shoulders a little in an attempt to remove such feelings from herself, Norah put a smile on her face and began to walk through St James' Park, praying that Lady Gillingham would be waiting as she had promised.

The last year had been something of a dull one and it brought Norah a good deal of pleasure to be back in town. Society had been severely lacking and the only other people in the world she had enjoyed conversation with had been her lady's maid, Cherry, and the housekeeper. Both had seemed to recognize that Norah was a little lonely and as the months had passed, a semblance of friendship – albeit a strange one – had begun to flourish. However, upon her return to town, Norah had been forced to leave both the maid and the housekeeper behind, for she was no longer permitted to reside in the small estate that had been hers for the last year. Now, she was to find a way to settle in London and with an entirely new complement of staff.

"Ah, Lady Essington! I am so glad to see you again."

Lady Gillingham rose quickly from where she had been seated on the small, wooden bench and, much to Norah's surprise, grasped her hands tightly whilst looking keenly into her eyes.

"I do hope you are well?"

Norah nodded, a prickling running down her spine. "I am quite well, I thank you."

"You have been looked after this past year?"

Opening her mouth to say that yes, she was quite satisfied, Norah slowly closed it again and saw the flicker of understanding in Lady Gillingham's eye.

"The newly titled Lord Essington did not wish for me to reside with him so I was sent to the dower house for the last few months," she explained, as Lady Gillingham's jaw tightened. "I believe that Lord Essington has spent the time attempting to find a way to remove from me what my late husband bequeathed but he has been unable to do so."

Lady Gillingham's eyes flared and a small smile touched the corner of her mouth. "I am very glad to hear it."

"I have a residence here in London and a small complement of staff." It was not quite the standard she was used to but Norah was determined to make the best of it. "I do not think I shall be able to purchase any new gowns - although it may be required of me somehow – but I am back in town, at the very least."

Lady Gillingham nodded, turned, and began to walk along the path, gesturing for Norah to fall into step with her. "You were given only a small yearly allowance?"

Norah shrugged one shoulder lightly. "It is more than enough to take care of my needs, certainly."

"But not enough to give you any real ease."

Tilting her head, Norah considered what she said, then chose to push away her pride and nod.

"It is as you say." There would be no additional expenses, no new gowns, gloves, or bonnets and she certainly could not eat extravagantly but at least she had a comfortable home. "The will stated that I was to have the furnished townhouse in London and that my brother-in-law is liable for all repairs to keep it to a specific standard for the rest of my remaining life and that, certainly, is a comfort."

"I can see that it is, although might you consider marrying again?"

Norah hesitated. "It is not something I have given a good deal of thought to, Lady Gillingham. I have had a great deal of loss these last few years, with the passing of my mother shortly after my marriage and, thereafter, the passing of Lord Essington himself. To find myself now back in London without a parent or husband is a little strange, and I confess that I find it a trifle odd. However, for the moment, it is a freedom that I wish to explore rather than remove from myself in place of another marriage."

Lady Gillingham laughed and the air around them seemed to brighten. "I quite understand. I, of course, never married again and there is not always a desire to do so, regardless. That is quite an understandable way of thinking and you must allow yourself time to become accustomed to your new situation."

"Yes, I think you are right."

Tilting her head slightly, Lady Gillingham looked sidelong at Norah. "And have you given any consideration to my proposal?"

Norah hesitated, her stomach dropping. Until this moment, she had been quite determined that she would *not* do as Lady Gillingham had asked, whereas now she was no longer as certain. Realizing she would have to live a somewhat frugal life for the rest of her days *or* marry a gentleman with a good deal more fortune – which was, of course, somewhat unlikely since she was a widow – the idea of earning a little more coin was an attractive one.

"I – I was about to refuse until this moment. But now that I am back in your company, I feel quite changed."

Lady Gillingham's eyes lit up. "Truthfully?"

Letting out a slightly awkward laugh, Norah nodded. "Although I am not certain I shall have the same way with words as you. How do you find such interesting stories?"

The burst of laughter that came from Lady Gillingham astonished Norah to the point that her steps slowed significantly.

"Oh, forgive me, Lady Essington! It is clear you have not plunged the depths of society as I have."

A slow flush of heat crept up Norah's cheeks. "It is true that I was very well protected from any belligerent gentlemen and the like. My mother was most fastidious."

"As she ought." Lady Gillingham attempted to hide her smile but it fought to remain on her lips. "But you shall find society a very different beast now, Lady Essington!"

Norah shivered, not certain that she liked that particular remark.

"You are a widowed lady, free to do as you please and act as you wish. You will find that both the gentlemen and ladies of the *ton* will treat you very differently now and that, Lady Essington, is where you will find all manner of stories being brought to your ears."

"I see."

A small frown pulled at Lady Gillingham's brow. "However, I made certain any stories I wrote had a basis in fact. I do not like to spread rumors unnecessarily. I stayed far from stories that would bring grave injury to certain parties."

Norah nodded slowly, seeing the frown and realizing just how seriously Lady Gillingham had taken her employment.

"There is a severe responsibility that must be considered before you take this on, Lady Essington. You must be aware that whatever you write *will* have consequences."

Pressing her lips together tightly, Norah thought about this for a few moments. "I recall that my mother and I used to read the society papers very carefully indeed, to make certain we would not keep company with any gentlemen who were considered poorly by the *ton*."

Lady Gillingham nodded. "Indeed, that is precisely what I mean. If a lady had been taken advantage of, then I would never write about her for fear of what that might entail. However, I would make mention of the gentleman in question, in some vague, yet disparaging, way that made certain to keep the rest of the debutantes away from him."

"I understand."

"We may not be well acquainted, Lady Essington, but I have been told of your kind and sweet nature by others. I believe they thought very well of your mother and, in turn, of you."

Norah put her hand to her heart, an ache in her throat. "I thank you."

Lady Gillingham smiled softly. "So what say you, Lady Essington? Will you do as I have long hoped?"

"Will I write under the name of Mrs. Fullerton?" A slow, soft smile pulled at her lips as she saw Lady

Gillingham nod. "And when would they wish their first piece?"

Lady Gillingham shrugged. "I write every week about what I have discovered. Sometimes the article is rather long and sometimes it is very short. The amount you write does not matter. It is what it contains that is of interest. They will pay you the same amount, regardless."

"They?" Norah pricked up her ears at the mention of money. "And might I ask how much is being offered?"

Norah's eyes widened as Lady Gillingham told her of the very large amount that would be given to her for every piece written. *That would allow me to purchase one new gown at the very least!*

"And it is the man in charge of the *London Chronicle* that has asked me for this weekly contribution. In time, you will be introduced to him. But that is only if you are willing to take on the role?"

Taking in a deep breath, Norah let it out slowly and closed her eyes for a moment. "Yes, I think I shall."

Lady Gillingham clapped her hands together in delight, startling a nearby blackbird. "How wonderful! I shall, of course, be glad to assist you with your first article. Thereafter, I fully intend to return to my house in the countryside and remain far away from *all* that London society has to offer." Her smile faded as she spoke, sending a stab of worry into Norah's heart. Could it be that after years of writing such articles, of being in amongst society and seeing all that went on, Lady Gillingham was weary of the *ton*? Norah swallowed hard and tried to push her doubts away. This was to bring her a little more coin and, therefore, a little more ease. After all that she had endured these last few years, that would be of the greatest comfort to her.

"So, when are you next to go into society?"

Norah looked at Lady Gillingham. "I have only just come to London. I believe I have an invitation to Lord Henderson's ball tomorrow evening, however."

"As have I." Lady Gillingham looped her arm through Norah's, as though they were suddenly great friends. "We shall attend together and I will help you find not only what you are to write about but I shall also introduce you to various gentlemen and ladies that you might wish to befriend."

A little confused, Norah frowned. "For what purpose?"

"Oh, some gentlemen, in particular, will have *excellent* potential when it comes to your writings. You do not have to like them – indeed, it is best if you do *not*, for your conscience's sake."

Norah's spirits dropped low. Was this truly the right thing for her to be doing? She did not want to injure gentlemen and ladies unnecessarily, nor did she want to have guilt on her conscience. *But the money would be so very helpful.*

"I can choose what I write, yes?"

Lady Gillingham glanced over at her sharply. "Yes, of course."

"And the newspaper will not require me to write any falsehoods?"

Lady Gillingham shook her head. "No, indeed not."

Norah set her shoulders. "Then I shall do as you have done and write what I think is only best for society to know, in order to protect debutantes and the like from any uncouth gentlemen."

"That is fair." Lady Gillingham smiled and Norah took in a long breath, allowing herself to smile as she settled the matter with her conscience. "I am sure you shall do very well indeed, Lady Essington."

Norah tilted her head up toward the sky for a moment as a sense of freedom burst over her once again. "I must hope so, Lady Gillingham. The ball will be a very interesting evening indeed, I am sure."

I THINK the society column will yield some very interesting stories, don't you? I hope Lady Essington does well! Check out the rest of the story in the Kindle Store The Truth about the Earl

JOIN MY MAILING LIST AND FACEBOOK READER GROUP

Sign up for my newsletter to stay up to date on new releases, contests, giveaways, freebies, and deals!

Free book with signup!

Monthly Facebook Giveaways! Books and Amazon gift cards!
Join my reader group on Facebook!

Rose's Ravenous Readers

Facebook Page: https://www.facebook.com/rosepearsonauthor

Website: www.RosePearsonAuthor.com
You can sign up for my Newsletter on my website too!

Follow me on Goodreads: Author Page

Printed in Great Britain
by Amazon